THE COMET FROM BEYOND THE UNKNOWN!

Inside the chilly gloom of the observatory, Bob Star sat down at the telescope. The great barrel swung to search space with its photoelectric eyes, and the pale beam of the projector flashed across to the concave screen.

Bob Star leaned to watch the screen. It was a well of darkness. White points danced in it. He found a patch of green, oddly blurred. He stepped up the electronic magnification. The comet swiftly grew.

Its shape was puzzling – a strangely perfect ellipsoid. A greenish football, he thought, kicked at the Solar System out of the night of space – by what?

'Twelve million miles long!' he muttered huskily. 'Which means it can't be any sort of solid matter. With that low density, it has to be hollow. *But what's inside?*' . . .

Also by Jack Williamson and available
from Sphere Books

THE LEGION OF SPACE (first in the Legion of Space series)
ONE AGAINST THE LEGION (third in the Legion of Space
series)

The Cometeers

The second novel
of the Legion of Space series

JACK WILLIAMSON

SPHERE BOOKS LIMITED
30/32 Gray's Inn Road, London WC1X 8JL

Published in Great Britain
by Sphere Books Ltd 1977
Copyright © 1950 by Jack Williamson
Magazine version copyright © 1936
by Street & Smith Publications, Inc.
Copyright © renewed 1964 by Jack Williamson
Published by arrangement with the author's agent

TRADE MARK

Set in Monotype Times

Printed in Great Britain by
C. Nicholls & Company Ltd
The Philips Park Press, Manchester

CONTENTS

Chapter One

THE PRISONER OF PHOBOS

Phobus spun on the time of Earth – for the ancient conquerors of that moonlet of Mars had adjusted its rotation to suit their imperial convenience. They had clad its dead stone with living green, and wrapped it in artificial air, and ruled the planets like captive islands from its palaces.

But their proud space navies had been beaten and forgotten long before these middle years of the thirtieth century. All the human islands around the sun were free again, and the youngest heir to the tarnished memories of that lost empire was a restless prisoner in the humbled Purple Hall.

Night was fading now into an ominous dawn, as the long crescent of Mars came up like a blood-rusted scimitar before the sun. Beneath its reddish light, a glass door slid open and he came out of the towering central pylon into the wide roof-garden on the western wing.

A slight young man, he wore the green of the Legion of Space, without any mark of rank or service decoration. With a frown of trouble on his boyish face, he paused to search the dark sky westward. Another man in green burst out of the door behind him.

'Bob Star! Where – ah, lad, there you are!' The older soldier of space was short and bald and fat, his tunic patched with the emblems of a long career but now unbuttoned in his haste. 'Can't you wait a moment for poor old Giles Habibula?'

'Sorry, Giles.' Bob Star turned quickly back, his thin, sunburned face warmed with a smile of amused affection for his panting bodyguard. 'I tried to slip away, but only for a glance at the sky. Must you follow every step I take?'

'You know I must,' the fat man puffed. 'Hal and I have your father's orders, to guard your life every instant with our own. And the great John Star is an officer who expects obedience.'

'The great John Star!' A momentary bitterness edged the young man's voice, before he saw the other's outraged loyalty. 'I suppose my father's really great.' He nodded soberly. 'I know he's the hero of a terrible war and the owner of Phobos and my mother's husband.

'But why must he have me guarded like a criminal?'

'Please, lad!' Giles Habibula came waddling anxiously to his side, through the transplanted shrubbery that made the garden a fragrant bit of the far-off Earth. 'Perhaps your father's sterner than old Giles would be, but he's only trying to make a soldier of you. And you know why you must be guarded.'

'For my own safety.' His trim shoulders lifted impatiently. 'So my father says. But I'm a graduate of the Legion Academy, with honours enough. I've been taught how to fight. Why can't he trust me to defend my own life, like anybody else?'

'But the stake is more than your life, lad.' Giles Habibula looked quickly about the empty walks, and drew him cautiously farther from the door. 'And your danger more than John Star's doing. It's no secret to Hal and me that you have been named by the Council to receive your mother's trust.'

Apprehension thinned Bob Star's brown face.

'You mean – AKKA?' His voice dropped with a wondering awe when he spoke of the mighty secret known by that brief symbol. The most precious possession of the united human planets, it was a weapon of most desperate resort, a power so awesome that each legal keeper of it was sworn to reveal it only to the next.

'That's your appointed duty, lad,' the old man was breathing solemnly. 'The noblest destiny a man can dream of – to be sole custodian of that great weapon, as your precious mother is. It was the order of the Council that you be guarded, from the day you were chosen. Hal and I are proud to serve you. Why fret about it?'

'But I'm not keeping any secret now,' he protested restlessly. 'None except the fact that my mother is to give me AKKA when her doctors say it's no longer safe with her – a day that I hope won't come for another twenty years and more. Must I stay a prisoner all the time I wait?'

'Perhaps the orders seem a trifle strict.' The old man's bald head bobbed sympathetically. 'But why fume about it? If we're confined to Phobos, it's still a precious scrap of paradise. We've all the comforts of the greatest palace in the system. To say nothing of the privilege of a noble cellar filled with famous vintages. Tell me, what's so mortal bad about it?'

'Nothing, really.' Bob Star's fingers lifted nervously to touch a scar on his forehead, a pale triangular ridge that didn't tan. 'I know it's a tremendous honour to be chosen keeper of AKKA, even though I didn't want it. But I couldn't sleep last night, and I suppose I got to brooding.'

'Your head?' Giles Habibula had seen his fingers on the scar. 'Is that the trouble, lad? Is that old concussion causing pain again?'

He dropped his hand self-consciously, his face drawn stern against the old man's sympathy. That throbbing pain had not come back – but only because it had never really ceased. The nature and the consequences of that old injury were secrets of his own, however, guarded as stubbornly as he meant to guard the weapon called AKKA. His lips tightened silently.

'If it's just a mood, I know the cure for that!' Giles Habibula beamed at him hopefully. 'A platter of ham and steak and eggs, with hot brown bread, and a pot of coffee to wash them down. And then perhaps an apple pie. You got up too mortal early, dragging a poor old soldier out of his bed without a blessed bite to eat. Let's go back to breakfast!'

'Later, Giles.' Bob Star spoke absently, peered at the dark sky again. 'But first I want to look for something.'

9

'Whatever it is, we'll never find it on an empty belly.' The old man was peering with a sudden dismay at the grim lines of strain, which made that searching face seem for a moment prematurely old. 'But what's the matter, lad? You're too young to look so grave.'

'I couldn't sleep,' Bob Star kept looking up at the sky. 'I don't quite know why. But my windows were open, and while I was lying there I happened to see something among the stars.'

'Yes, lad?' The wheezy voice of Giles Habibula seemed curiously apprehensive. 'And what was that?'

'Just a little greenish fleck,' Bob Star said slowly. 'In Virgo, near Vindemiatrix. I don't quite know why, but it got on my nerves. It went out of sight, when Mars began to rise. I don't know what it was, but I'm going to have a look at it, with the telescope yonder.'

He started on toward the shining dome of the small observatory he had set up at the end of the garden – so that he could rove the stars with its electronic screens and his own restless mind, in spite of his imprisonment.

'Wait, lad!' The fat man's voice was sharper. 'You wouldn't drag a poor old soldier of the Legion out of his blessed sleep in the middle of the night, just to look at a star?'

'But it isn't an ordinary star.' He swung back to Giles Habibula, with a frown of disturbed perplexity. 'Because I know it wasn't there a few nights ago – I happened to be searching that same sector of the sky for an asteroid that seems to have strayed off the charts. It couldn't be a nova – not with that strange, pale green colour!'

'Forget it, lad,' the old Legionnaire whined persuasively. 'Any star can have a wicked look, to a man without his breakfast.'

'I don't know what to think.' He shook his head uneasily. 'The object got to haunting me, while I lay there watching it. It got to seeming like an eye, staring back. It made me – afraid.' He shivered, in the thin wind across the roof. 'I don't know why, but I am really afraid.'

'Afraid?' Giles Habibula gave the brightening sky a hurried, fishy glance. 'I don't see anything to fear. And we're no cowards, lad. Neither you nor I. Not with the proper victuals in us—'

'Perhaps it's a comet.' Still frowning, Bob Star swung back towards the observatory. 'It looked like one – it was a short streak of that queer, misty green, instead of the point a star would show.'

He shrugged uncomfortably.

'But then any comet should have been detected and reported long ago, by the big observatories. It hasn't been – I've been reading all the astrophysical reports, with nothing else to do! I can't imagine what it is, but I'm going to have a look.'

'Don't, lad!' The wheezy voice sharpened, with a puzzling urgency. 'Let's not meddle with fate.'

'How's that?' He peered sharply at the old man's seamed bland face. 'What's wrong with you?'

'I've seen trouble – and I don't like it.' Giles Habibula nodded unhappily. 'I know we've had a peaceful time this last year, since Hal and I came back with you from Earth. Ah, a happy time, with little to do but fill our guts and sleep. But I've lived through things to chill your blood.'

Bob Star backed away, watching him anxiously.

'I've known the mortal times some men call adventure,' he went on dolefully. 'I was with your father, along with Commander Kalam and Hal Samdu, twenty years and more ago, when we went out to the Runaway Star, to fight the wicked Medusae for your dear mother's life and her precious secret.'

'I know.' Bob Star nodded. 'The four of you were the heroes who rescued my mother's weapon and saved the human planets. But what has that to do with this fleck of green mist in the sky?'

'Only that I've had enough,' the old man said. 'Listen lad, to a word of kind advice. Heroism is damned uncomfortable. Let's forget this monstrous comet. It might have waited until my poor old bones were laid to rest –

instead of coming to upset my last days with such frightful talk.'

He shook his head forebodingly.

'Poor old Giles! He had only sat down, with a bottle of wine in his trembling fingers, ready to stretch his legs before the fire and doze away into the last blessed sleep, when this fearful comet came, to start him awake with the threat of another stellar war. Ah, in dear life's name –'

'Stellar war!' Bob Star seized the old man's pudgy arm. 'Then the danger isn't just imagination?' His hard fingers tightened. 'And you knew about that green comet – how long ago?'

The old man squirmed and shook his head.

'No, no, lad!' he muttered hastily. 'There's nothing at all to worry about, not here on Phobos. You just dragged me out of sleep too mortal sudden. My poor old wits are still fogged and groggy. You must pay no heed, lad, to the babblings of a battle-shaken veteran of the Legion.'

'What about the comet?'

'Please, lad! I know nothing. In life's name –'

'It's too late, Giles.' His fingers sank deeper. 'You've already talked too much. If you don't want to tell me what this is all about – and why it's being kept from me – I can ask some awkward questions.'

'Then stop it, lad!' the old man moaned. 'You needn't shake me like a dying rat.'

Waiting breathlessly, Bob Star released his arm.

'A whisper in the Legion. I've no secrets of the Council, lad. And it was your own father who ordered us to keep it from you. You won't let on that old Giles breathed a word about it?'

'My own father!' Bitterness heightened Bob Star's anxiety. 'He thinks I'm a weakling and a coward.'

'Not so, lad,' muttered Giles Habibula. 'He was just afraid the worry of it, and the mortal shock, might be too much for you.'

'He doesn't trust me,' Bob Star whispered. 'But tell me about this comet – if that's what it is.'

'I've your promise, lad, not to tell him?'

'I promise,' Bob Star said. 'Go on.'

Cautiously, the old soldier drew him across the grass, into the shelter of a clump of white-flowering frangipani. He glanced uneasily about the great roof, and up at the mighty central tower of the Purple Hall, which was already ablaze in the sunlight above them.

'The fearful thing was first seen ten weeks ago.' His nasal voice sank to a hissing whisper. 'Picked up by the great free-space observatory at Contra-Saturn Station. It was plunging toward the Solar System, with a velocity that threw the astronomers into fits.'

He caught apprehensively at Bob Star's arm.

'But you'll remember, lad? You'll not give poor old Giles away, for the stupid blunder of his tongue? Your father's a stern man. Even though he and I are comrades of that great voyage to the Runaway Star. – You'll remember?'

'I keep my word,' Bob Star said. 'But what's so alarming about this comet?'

'It's like no other,' the old man wheezed. 'It's no frail thing of pebbles and ionized gas, and it's larger than any other comet ever was. The astronomers don't know what it is. But it's twelve million miles long, lad – imagine that! And it has a thousand times the mass of Earth. It can't be any member of the System, they say. A strange body, driving out of the black gulf of space amid the stars.'

Bob Star had drawn back dazedly.

'I see,' he whispered huskily. 'And what else about it?'

'The astronomers are tearing out their hair, lad. So your father told us. Because the thing has upset all their calculations. Its motion is all wrong. When the pull of the sun should have begun to increase its speed – it stopped!'

The old man's shifty, red-rimmed eyes looked quickly out across the garden, and up at the dark sky, and hastily back at Bob Star again. It shook him to see that Giles Habibula was frightened.

'What stopped it?'

'Nobody in the System knows.' The rusty voice dropped lower. 'Now it's just hanging there. Five billion miles out – far beyond Pluto! That isn't the motion of any kind of comet, Bob. A space ship might stop that way – if you can imagine a space ship twelve million miles long!'

'What else?' Bob Star stood taut with a mixture of dread and excitement. 'What's happened since?'

'That's all I know – except that the Council is alarmed. You can't blame 'em! That's why your father was called to Earth, to meet with them at the Green Hall. They've ordered a censorship on any news about the comet – as if the people can't be hurt by a military secret!'

'I wonder what they're planning?'

'That's top secret, but I know the talk of the Legion.' The old man turned to glance furtively behind him again. 'I suppose you've heard of the *Invincible*?'

'The new battleship?'

'The greatest ship the System ever built.' Giles Habibula beamed with a momentary pride. 'A thousand feet long, and armed with a vortex gun – the great new weapon that won our war with Stephen Orco. A thing almost as dreadful as your mother's secret device.'

'I know,' Bob Star whispered impatiently. 'But what about it?'

'I've no high secrets, lad,' the old voice rasped. 'All I know is the talk of the Legion. But I hear the *Invincible* is to carry some sort of expedition out to discover what's inside that green cloud – to operate the comet like a ship!'

Fat fingers tugged again at Bob Star's sleeve.

'You'll remember, lad?' Giles Habibula begged. 'You won't tell your father?'

Bob Star stood very straight in that undecorated uniform, his dark head uncovered to the cold and distant sun rising now beneath the fading scimitar of Mars. The fingers of his right hand were tracing, as they often did, the triangular scar on his forehead. His tanned face was bleakly set.

'Don't worry, Giles,' he said quietly. 'I won't tell.'

Abruptly, then, he exploded: 'So my father told you to keep it from me? He's afraid I couldn't stand the shock! Why doesn't he order you to rock me to sleep in your lap?'

Chapter Two

THE KEEPER OF THE PEACE

Bob Star hurried on again toward the observatory dome. Giles Habibula limped hastily after him, peering at the dark sky and starting at every rustle of the wind in the shrubbery, as if his fishy eyes had already seen some unpleasant visitant descending from the comet to the roof.

Outside the little dome, Bob Star paused. He stood at the end of the roof, beside a low parapet of purple glass. Far beneath lay Phobos – a moonlet so tiny and so rugged that it seemed like a solitary mountain peak beneath the palace, floating alone in space, detached from any world at all. Yet it was green with transplanted forests, and spangled with artificial lakes.

He could remember when it had been large enough, and lovely to him, a dazzling triumph of the planetary engineers, its narrow valleys filled with all the adventure he could seek. But that was in his boyhood, before he went away to the Legion Academy. It was just a prison to him now.

Giles Habibula sat down on a bench in the sun. He fumbled in the pockets of his unbuttoned uniform and found a little empty flask, with a graduated scale along the side. He held it up to the sunlight and his eyes dwelt gloomily upon a single lonely drop of the wine he loved.

'Go on, lad,' he whispered sadly. 'If you must look into the ghastly face of death! Poor old Giles will wait here for you. He's good for nothing now, but to roast his aching bones in the sun.'

Inside the chilly gloom of the observatory, Bob Star sat down at the telescope. Its mechanism whirred softly, in swift response to his touch. The great barrel swung to search space with its photoelectric eyes, and the pale beam of the projector flashed across to the concave screen.

Bob Star leaned to watch the screen. It was a well of darkness. White points danced in it. The brightest, he knew, was the third-magnitude star Vindemiatrix. Near it he found a patch of pallid green, oddly blurred.

He stepped up the electronic magnification. Vindemiatrix and the fainter stars slipped out of the field. The comet hung alone, and swiftly grew. Its shape was puzzling – a strangely perfect ellipsoid. A greenish football, he thought, kicked at the System out of the night of space – by what?

'Twelve million miles long!' he muttered huskily. 'Which means it can't be any sort of solid matter. With that low density, it has to be hollow. But what's inside?'

Using ray filters and spectroscope, with the full power of the circuits, he strove to pierce that dull green veil, and failed. He sprang to his feet and stopped the instrument, impatiently snapping his fingers. Outside, he walked heavily to where Giles Habibula sat.

'It's no use,' he muttered. 'I found the cloud around it, but I failed to see inside. Nothing gets through – not a ray!'

He shivered again. For he had never seen anything so bafflingly weird, so strangely terrible. The comet was dreadful with the forbidden mystery of the dark interstellar wastes from which it had come, and its very vastness overwhelmed his mind. It was something beyond the range and scale of men, as men are beyond the microscopic infusorians swarming in a water-drop.

'Well, lad, you've seen it.' Giles Habibula was rolling cheerfully to his feet. 'The best astronomers in the System have done no more. Let's eat, before we perish.'

Bob Star nodded silently, his mind still numb with consternation. They were halfway back across the roof, when the old soldier paused, pointing westward as abruptly as if he had seen the comet,

Turning, Bob Star saw a white arrow with a head of pale blue flame. It wheeled above the rusty crescent of Mars, and grew in the sky. A rustling whisper came into the air. The shrubbery shook to a roaring gale of sound. A silver spindle flashed overhead, so near that he could see the black dots of observation ports, and recognise the *Phantom Star*.

'My father!' He felt the roof quiver faintly, as the landing ship came down on the great stage that topped the central tower. 'He'll know all about the comet, and what the Green Hall has done.'

'Your mother is waiting in the Jade Room,' a guard in the corridor told Bob Star. 'There was an ultrawave message from John Star. He's coming to meet her there.'

The Jade Room was enormous, its high walls panelled with jade-green glass and polished silver. On two sides, vast windows overlooked the darker green and brighter silver of the landscaped moonlet. The floor and the massive furnishings were of Venusian hardwoods, shining ruby-red.

His mother, she who had been Aladoree Anthar, sat quietly in a great chair that made her seem almost tiny. She looked up as he came in, and a quick smile brushed the pale trouble from her face. He could guess how grave her thoughts had been, but she said only:

'You're up early, son.'

He paused inside the door, feeling painfully awkward. She was very lovely and he knew she intended to be kind. Yet, when anything reminded him of her great trust, she became a personage, too aloof and great to be his mother. He asked nervously:

'Father's coming here?'

'He just landed.' Her breathless gladness made her seem human again. It made him want to run to her and put his arms around her. Somehow it filled his eyes with tears. He had started impulsively toward her, when he heard what she was saying:

'Your father sent a message ahead to ask me to wait for him here, alone. Perhaps you had better go outside, Bob, for just a few minutes.'

That stopped him. He stood looking at her. His fingers were twisting savagely at a button on the front of his tunic.

It came off in his hand, and he glanced down at it blankly.

'Why, Bob!' His mother came quickly toward him from her throne-like chair. 'Is something wrong? What makes you look so strange?' She caught his arm gently. 'You're shaking. Are you ill?'

He shook his head, blinking angrily at his tears.

'I'm all right,' he muttered huskily. 'If you didn't treat me this way!'

'Bob!' Her face looked hurt. 'I didn't mean to seem unkind–'

'You're too kind!' he broke in harshly. 'But I want to be trusted. I want a chance to live – even if it means a chance of getting killed. I can't stand to be shut up here, when things are happening.' He caught a sobbing breath. 'If you want to be really kind, send me out to explore the comet on the *Invincible*.'

She stepped back quickly, her face suddenly pale.

'I didn't know you knew,' she whispered. For a moment she was silent, and then she shook her head regretfully. 'I'm sorry, Bob,' she said. 'I had no idea you felt this way. John and I are very proud that you were chosen to be the next keeper of the peace.' She looked at him anxiously. 'Doesn't that promise you danger enough?'

'But how can I ever learn to face danger?' he demanded bleakly. 'If you and father keep on treating me like a child. Guarding me like a prisoner!'

'I hope we haven't sheltered you too much.' Moving closer to him, she seemed to hesitate. 'There – there's something I'd better tell you, Bob.'

He stiffened, at the sudden gravity of her voice.

'You know you made a very brilliant record at the academy, Bob – your father and I are very proud of that. Only one student ever finished with a higher average. He was Stephen Orco.'

He winced from that name, his fingers drifting instinctively toward the scar on his forehead.

'When you graduated, Bob, the commanding officer told us he was worried about you. He thought you had driven yourself too hard, trying to beat Orco's marks. He showed us a report from the staff doctors. They agreed that you were near a nervous breakdown, and they advised a year of complete rest for you before you were given any duty. He warned us not to tell you about the report until you were better.'

She smiled at him hopefully.

'I'm sure you're all right now,' she said. 'But that's why you've been here.'

Bob Star was staring past her, at the windows and the ragged near horizon.

'It wasn't overwork that hurt me,' he whispered faintly. 'It was Stephen Orco—'

But his mother wasn't listening. He turned, and saw that his father had entered the room. John Star came striding across the wide red floor, trim and straight as always in the green of the Legion. Hard and slender, he looked little older than his son. He came straight to Aladoree, and administered a brief soldierly kiss, and handed her a heavy, sealed envelope.

'Darling,' he said, 'this is an order from the Green Hall Council.' Gravely preoccupied, he turned to his son. 'Robert,' he said, 'I wish to see your mother alone.'

Bob Star stood speechless. The jade-green walls were cold as ice. The red floor was a terrible emptiness. His knees were going to buckle, and he had nothing to hold to.

'Please, sir—' His dry throat stuck.

'Let him stay, John,' his mother said quickly.

'If it's about the comet,' he muttered hoarsely, 'I've already seen it.'

'It is.' John Star looked at Aladoree, and nodded abruptly. 'You may sit down, Robert.'

He collapsed gratefully into a great chair and clung to the cold red hardwood, trying to stop the trembling of his hands. He saw his mother's wide grey eyes lift slowly toward John Star, from the document she had taken from the envelope. Her face was white with incredulous dismay.

20

'John.' Her voice was very quiet. 'This is an order for me to destroy the object in Virgo, at once, with AKKA.'

John Star's nod had a military severity.

'The resolution to destroy the cometary object was approved by the Council eight hours ago,' he said briskly. 'I brought the order to you at the full speed of the *Phantom Star* – a record crossing.'

The big grey eyes rested for a time on John Star's face.

'John,' his mother asked very softly, 'do you know what you are asking me to do?'

'Certainly.' John Star looked at her with an annoyed impatience. 'I spoke before the Council in favour of the motion. The vote was very close. There were sentimental objections.'

'Perhaps I'm sentimental,' she answered quickly. 'But I don't want to destroy that object – not unless we must. Because it's something very wonderful – so wonderful that none of our scientists will undertake to say what it is.'

She stepped quickly toward him.

'Can we just erase it from existence, without ever knowing?'

'We can – we must!' Still standing, John Star had drawn his lean body very straight. 'Consider the arguments for the destruction of that unknown object and the beings who appear to operate it like a ship – the news reporters had coined a word for them, before we set up the censorship. The Cometeers!

'Their science must be immensely ahead of our own – except that they probably don't possess your weapon. And their hostility is as certain as their power!'

An oratorical ring had come into John Star's voice, as if he were quoting phrases from his talk before the Council.

'On Earth, everywhere in the System, the law of survival has set even the most closely kindred forms of life to killing one another. The Cometeers can't be our kinsmen, in any degree – they may be something we couldn't recognize as life at all.

'Logically, they must be our enemies.

21

'The peculiar motion of the cometary object is itself sufficient evidence of some purpose in relation to our planets. That purpose is necessarily for the benefit of the Cometeers, because they are ovbiously a successful and hence a selfish type of life – however they may look!'

Aladoree was shaking her head.

'I'm not so sure of your logic.'

'Then sentimentalists in the Council tried to question it,' John Star answered. 'Fortunately, the Cometeers have already given us more convincing evidence of their hostile intentions.'

He paused dramatically, and Aladoree asked softly:

'How is that, John?'

'They have actually visited most of our planets.'

'People,' Bob Star broke in, 'have actually *seen* them?'

'Not exactly.' John Star didn't look away from his wife. 'The creatures of the comet are – or made themselves for the occasion of their visits – invisible. But they've left signs enough.'

Aladoree asked quickly, 'What have they done?'

'They came in some massive machine, whose drive-fields were powerful enough to disturb our ultrawave communications. Evidently their first object was to investigate our defences – the invisible ship always landed near some Legion stronghold. On Earth, twenty-four hours ago, the raiders killed four guards – with a frightful weapon. They entered a locked vault, which we had thought impregnable. They escaped with a precious military secret.'

John Star stepped quickly toward his wife. Suddenly he was no longer the soldier and orator, but only a man, anxiously begging.

'Please darling!' he whispered. 'I know you have the right to veto the first order. And I know what a terrible responsibility you carry. I think I understand your feelings. But this danger's too great and near to be denied. For all we know, one of the invisible Cometeers may be with us now, in this very room!'

He glanced quickly about that jade-and-silver chamber.

Agony whitened his lean face, and tears shone in his eyes. Impulsively, he swept Aladoree into his arms. Bob Star stepped quickly back, astonished, he had almost forgotten that his father was a human being, as well as a soldier.

'Won't you do it, darling?' he was pleading. 'For your sake – and for mine!'

Gravely, Aladoree pushed his arms away.

'What was the secret,' she asked, 'that the Cometeers got?'

John Star turned to look at his son. His lips drew tight. He nodded slowly, as if in reluctant admission of Bob's right to be there.

'They learned,' he said, 'that the man known as Merrin is still alive.'

Bob Star watched the new dismay that swept the colour from his mother's face. He saw the slight, shocked movement of her head. Her voice, when at last she spoke, seemed oddly quiet.

'It makes all the difference, if they know about – about Merrin. It leaves us no choice.' She nodded unwillingly. 'If they've found out – that, then they must be destroyed.'

Chapter Three

THE FULCRUM AND THE FORCE

Bob Star stood watching his mother, frowning with a puzzled anxiety. With the stern regret with which she had made that terrible decision still lingering on her face, she had turned quickly away from him and his father. She was bent now over a small table of polished Venusian scarletwood, busy with a few little objects she had gathered from about her person: her watch, a pen and a mechanical pencil, a metal ornament from her dress, an iron key.

'Must I go?' he whispered.

She looked up at him, with a grave little smile.

'You may stay,' she said. 'Since one day you are to become the keeper of the peace. Though there's very little to see.' She glanced at the harmless-seeming objects on the little table. 'You could watch a thousand times without learning the secret,' she added, 'because the control of AKKA is more than half mental.'

She was busy again. With a deft skill that seemed to show long practice, she unscrewed the barrel from the pen and removed two tiny perforated discs from the back of the watch. Upon the mechanical pencil, whose working parts provided a fine adjustment, she began assembling a tiny, odd-looking contrivance. The platinum chain of the ornament seemed to form an electrical connection, and the clip from the pen would function as a key.

Bob Star peered at it, and whispered unbelievingly.

'Is that little gadget – all there is?'

'It's all there is to see.' Her fine eyes came back to him for an instant, frowning with the gravity of her task. 'This little device is merely the lever,' she said. 'The force that moves it is mental. The fulcrum on which it works –' Her pale lips grew stern. 'The fulcrum is the secret.'

Bob Star shook his head, staring at that tiny instrument.

'You mean that you destroyed the Moon, when those other invaders from the Runaway Star had made their fortress there – with only that for a weapon?'

'With the same sort of lever.' She glanced at John Star, and he gave her an awed little smile, as if they both were living again through that dreadful instant. 'I made that one from bits of wreckage from the bombed Green Hall, and parts of a broken toy.'

Bob Star leaned closer, dazedly.

'It seems impossible that you could destroy anything so vast as the comet – with only that!'

'Size doesn't matter,' she said quietly. 'Neither does distance. This little device you see is only the lever, remember, through which that force can be applied to any object in the universe.' She glanced up again, still frowning with her preoccupation. 'The effect is a fundamental, absolute change in the warp of space, which reduces matter and energy alike to impossible absurdities.'

Bob Star was silent for a moment, breathless. He shrank back a little, shaken with a startled dread, from this gravely smiling woman. She was his mother no longer, but something as strange and terrible as the Cometeers must be. Shining on her face was a calm, passionless serenity.

'Mother – mother,' he whispered huskily. 'You're like – like a goddess!'

It seemed strange that she should hear him, in her remote detachment. But she turned to him soberly, and said: 'It's lonely, Bob – being a goddess.'

Her eyes left him. For a few moments she worked in silence, assembling the device. But presently she paused again, to look up at him.

'Bob, there's one thing you ought to know now, since you've been chosen to be the next keeper. That's the reason there must be only one keeper – the reason you must wait for the secret, until the doctors find that it is no longer safe with me.'

He stood listening, cold with a troubled expectation.

'There is one limitation to the use of AKKA.' She hesitated, frowning at him soberly. 'Even the existence of that limitation is a high secret, which you must not repeat.'

He nodded, waiting breathlessly.

'To use the same figure of speech,' she said quietly, 'there is only one fulcrum.'

'Huh?' His breath caught. 'I don't understand.'

'There's just one fulcrum,' she repeated quietly. 'That is not a literal statement, but it's all I can say before you are to be entrusted with the secret. What you must understand is simply this: If two people know the secret, and try to use their levers at the same time, neither can succeed. It would be entirely useless to the two of us, if we tried to use it independently.'

'I see.' He stepped toward her quickly, moved by a sudden dread. '"What happens to you?' he whispered sharply. 'After you have told me?'

'Nothing painful.' Her grey eyes looked up again, shining with a serenity that he couldn't understand. 'You can see that the knowledge must not be left where it might be unsafe.'

'You mean –' He knew what she meant, but suddenly he couldn't say the words. 'Aren't you afraid?'

She shook her head. To his amazement, she was smiling.

'I don't mind,' she whispered softly. 'You won't, after you have been the keeper of the peace as long as I have. I suppose that last duty of the keeper must seem a terrible penalty, to you today. But there comes a time when you see that it is the final, most fitting and most precious reward for our special service.'

'I – I can't see that.' That waiting duty became suddenly vast and dreadful in his mind, and he felt small with a new humility. 'But I'm sorry – mother.' He reached out to touch her arm with a diffident caress. 'I'm sorry I've been

26

fretting so – about waiting here with nothing much to do.'

She reached to catch his hand and squeeze it sympathetically, and then stooped quickly again over the queerly toy-like device on the little table, which was a lever to thrust whole planets into annihilation. When he saw the look on her face – the calm authority that was almost divine and the willing acceptance of ultimate death as its price – his own restless impatience began to seem petty childishness. She finished some final adjustment, and straightened to face John Star.

'It's ready,' she said.

'Then use it.'

She picked up the tiny device, and carried it to the vast west windows. Following, Bob Star was shaken with a puzzled dread. He wet his lips, and whispered hoarsely:

'Can you use it safely, here inside the building? And find the comet, without a telescope?'

'I can.' She glanced back gravely. 'It's mental force, that moves the lever. There's no danger to anything except the object at which it is directed. And a telescope would be only in the way, because light's too slow to show the target where it is. What I've called the fulcrum, remember, is something outside space and time.'

She had turned to lift the small device, her slender hands white with her tension but yet oddly steady. She seemed to be sighting through the peepholes in the two tiny metal discs – though the comet, now by day, was invisible to Bob Star's eyes. Her finger was moving to touch the key when John Star sprang to catch her arm.

'Wait!' he gasped.

Beyond them, Bob Star saw a pale blur of blue flame in the sky. He heard the whisper and the rushing and the thunderous roar of rockets. The air was alive with quivering sound, and he glimpsed a mountain of white metal, flashing above the window. Then the red floor trembled, and the rockets were suddenly still.

'It's the *Invincible*!' In that abrupt silence, John Star's taut voice seemed oddly small and far away. 'Commander Kalam must have followed me – I can't quite imagine why!' He turned slowly from the window, to Aladoree. 'I think you should wait, until we know.'

Bob Star had run to join them at the window. A thousand feet below and a mile away, he saw the enormous ship – far too large for the stage on the tower, it had come down in the forest. The trees beyond it were uprooted and blazing from the rocket blast.

Even from this height, it looked literally invincible, and the shining might of it gave him a momentary sense of pride in the Legion and mankind. It was the most magnificent machine that men had ever made. The geodyne drive put the stars within its reach. New, refractory alloys made its bright hull invulnerable. Its great weapon, the atomic vortex gun, could desolate planets.

A rocket plane lifted from the hull, as he watched, and climbed swiftly towards the stage above the tower. His mother's eyes followed it, bright with hope.

'That must be Jay,' she whispered. 'We must wait.'

She lowered the device she had been aiming towards the comet, and Bob Star turned from the mighty miracle of the *Invincible* to peer at it once more.

'It's so small!' he protested breathlessly. 'Made of such common things! It looks so insignificant – beside the *Invincible*. As if it couldn't really destroy – anything!'

'This is only the lever.' She lifted it on her small palm, almost casually. She must have seen the awed wonder in his eyes, for she added quietly: 'I carry it taken apart and the parts disguised, as another measure of security. Yet, even if the assembled instrument fell into hostile hands, there would be no danger. No manipulation of the instrument itself can have any effect, unless you know the fulcrum and the force.'

Bob Star came to attention, with a quick salute, when Jay Kalam entered the room. Oddly, although he had been commander of the Legion for nearly twenty years, he looked far less soldierly than John Star. He was slender and dark and tall, with no trace of military stiffness in his bearing. His green-and-gold uniform was worn with a confident assurance, but it failed to disguise the grave reserve of the scholarly gentleman.

'John!' He spoke from the doorway, his voice quick with urgency. 'Aladoree! Have you destroyed the object in Virgo?'

She moved toward him anxiously.

'Not yet,' she whispered. 'In another second – but we saw your rockets –'

'Then don't!' His thin face relaxed, and the breath sighed out of him. He came on into the room, smiling slightly now. 'I was afraid I had got here too late,' he said huskily. 'The Council has rescinded its order –'

'What's that?' John Star's voice was brittle as the snap of breaking glass. 'Why?'

Deliberately, the tall man drew another heavy envelope from an inside pocket of his tunic, and handed it gravely to Aladoree. She opened it hastily, and her grey eyes smiled again as she read the document.

'I'm glad you got here, Jay,' she whispered softly. 'You have saved me from murdering – something that must be very wonderful!'

'Why is this?' John Star's lips were tight, his narrow face pale and stern. 'Why was the order rescinded?'

The grave commander of the Legion swung quietly towards him.

'John,' he said soberly, 'you know the Council was divided on ordering the destruction of the cometary object. I myself opposed it – as the murder of something greater than a planet. After you departed, I got permission to speak before the Council, in favour of a more moderate policy.'

'But – Jay!' John Star's voice was sharp with his apprehensive urgency. 'We know already that the Cometeers are hostile. We know they've found out about Merrin. Every moment the comet exists increases our danger. It must be destroyed!'

The tall commander shook his head.

'I know your arguments, John,' he said slowly. 'And we all admit that the situation is extremely grave. We must take stern measures to assure the safety of the System. But we aren't justified yet, in annihilating the object – without even finding out what it really is. While it's true that the Cometeers have been scouting our military establishments, it's quite possible that they are only trying to protect themselves from the hasty use of some such weapon as Aladoree's. For all we know, their purpose in approaching the System may be entirely peaceful.'

'Jay, you're a pacifist at heart.' Restrained anger cracked in John Star's voice. 'You've no business in the Legion!'

'I'll not be guilty of the murder of an unknown world,' Jay Kalam answered softly. 'Not just out of panic. My business in the Legion is the protection of civilization – and what does that mean, without justice or mercy? If we attempt the needless destruction of the comet, I feel that we're asking for the same sort of fate.

'Anyhow, John, I was able to convince several members of the Council that they had been unduly swayed by your war talk. The first motion was to send an ultrawave message to call you back, but I pointed out the probability that the Cometeers might intercept and decode the order. I could see an actual danger there – because I can feel the weight of your arguments, John, even though I favour moderation. You had been gone only two hours, and I thought we could overtake you with the *Invincible*. It seems we were nearly too late.'

'You'll wish you had been too late.' John Star's face looked pale and rigid, and his voice sounded hoarse and stern and terrible. 'And the System will!' He nodded bleakly at the document Jay Kalam had brought. 'That paper is the death-warrant for mankind.'

An ominous quiet hung in the Jade Room. Silently, at last, Aladoree walked back to the scarletwood table and stooped to take apart her harmless-seeming weapon.

'I hope you're wrong, John,' Jay Kalam said.

'But I'm not,' John Star answered flatly. 'I've no desire to be needlessly ruthless. But my duty is to guard the keeper of the peace, and I can't afford to let mistaken emotions stand in the way. I know this, Jay: by saving the comet you are murdering the System.'

Chapter Four

THE MAN CALLED MERRIN

A terrible taut stillness reigned for a little while in the Jade Room. John Star stood motionless and alone on the vast red floor, his pale face set like a mask of death. Something made the others shrink back from him.

Bob Star heard the sudden catch in his father's breath, and saw the wet glitter in his eyes. The guardian of the keeper was suddenly also a man defending his wife. He strode to Aladoree and turned, with his arm around her waist, to look almost defiantly at the commander of the Legion.

'Well, Jay?' His voice was flat and hard and dry. 'If we can't destroy the comet, what are we going to do?'

'The Green Hall voted to leave that in my hands,' Jay Kalam said. 'I considered the situation carefully, while we came out from Earth. I've worked out a plan that I think is safe.'

'Yes?' John Star waited, grimly intent.

'There are three things we must do,' the lean commander said deliberately. 'We must protect the keeper. We must guard the prisoner known as Merrin. We must find out as soon as possible whether the existence of the comet is any actual danger to the System.

'The first task is your duty, John.'

John Star nodded silently, his arm drawing tighter around Aladoree.

'But I doubt that she's safe any longer, here in the Purple Hall,' Jay Kalam added. 'Phobos is well defended – but so was that vault in the Green Hall, which the Cometeers raided. With their invisibility, they would probably be able to land and enter the building, undetected. What was left of the men guarding that vault shows that they have strange and terrible weapons.'

32

'I'm quite aware of that!'

'Then I suggest that you take Aladoree away from here, on the *Phantom Star*, at once. I don't want to know where. You may select your own destination. Keep it secret. You can send some member of the Council the necessary information about how to communicate with you, if it does become necessary to use AKKA – a simple set of code signals, for ultrawave broadcast, ought to be sufficient.'

'Yes, sir,' John Star gave him a brisk salute.

'The defences of the man called Merrin,' he continued deliberately, 'are already as good as the Legion can make them – except in one particular. I'm going to call upon your son, to make them complete.'

He turned to Bob Star, his dark eyes searchingly intent.

'Are you ready, Bob, to undertake a very important and very dangerous duty, for the Legion and the System?'

'Yes – yes, sir!' Bob Star's voice tried to stick, but he was trembling with an incredulous joy. Dismay shook him, when he heard his father's quick protest.

'Robert isn't ready for duty,' John Star said. 'I was planning to take him with us, when we leave on the *Phantom Star*.'

'No!' Bob Star gasped. 'Please – I want something to do.'

John Star merely shrugged at that, but Aladoree caught his arm.

'Bob and I have been talking, John,' she said quickly. 'He feels that we have been shielding him too much, and I believe he's right. I think he really needs a chance to prove himself.'

'Thank you, mother!' Bob Star whispered, and he turned eagerly to the grave commander. 'Please – I want to try – whatever I can do. I want to try – and I'll do my best!'

'This will need your best.' And Jay Kalam turned to John Star. 'John,' he said quietly, 'for this service I must call upon your son. No other man will do. You recall the adjustment of the Jovian Revolt. There's the matter of a promise given – and I intend to respect the honour of the Legion, even in such times as these.'

John Star turned slowly back to his son. Watching him uneasily, Bob could see the stern reflection of some searching question on his face, but at last he nodded, without ever asking it. He swung back abruptly to Jay Kalam.

'Yes, I suppose we must go on keeping our word.' His voice seemed cold and harsh. 'You may give Robert the necessary orders.'

Bob Star felt an ache in his throat. He wanted to thank his father, but the bleak set of John Star's face checked the words. He lifted his arm in an impulsive salute, and John Star returned it stiffly.

'For the third matter,' Jay Kalam said again, 'I am going out to the object in Virgo, on the *Invincible*. We shall keep in contact with the Green Hall, so long as possible, with tight-beam ultrawave. I intend to discover the true nature of the object and the purpose of its enigmatic motion. I hope to find that it isn't quite so dangerous as you think.'

John Star stepped forward quickly, and shook the commander's hand. He seemed to swallow, and then said huskily, 'Jay!'

'I fully expect to be seeing you again, John,' Jay Kalam said evenly. 'If we don't return, however, I suppose it will be advisable to destroy the object. It will take us about five days to reach it and five to return. Give us two more. If we haven't come back in twelve days, John, you may consider us lost – and forget my protests against destroying the object.'

He paused, turning to Bob Star.

'Bob, you will come with us on the *Invincible* to the prison of the man known as Merrin. We'll have time on the crossing for me to explain the details and the great importance of your duty. You may make your farewells. We are leaving at once.'

Bob Star turned breathlessly toward his mother.

His father was beckoning the commander aside. 'Jay, I've decided where to look for our new sanctuary. We'll be leaving Phobos within two hours. As for communication –'

Cautiously, John Star lowered his voice.

The woman who was also the keeper of the peace moved quickly to meet her son. Her tall loveliness caught his heart with a sharp pang of yearning affection, and the tender softness of her voice, when she spoke, brought back to him all the bittersweet of childhood. She took both his hands in hers, and drew him to her with a quivering urgency. Her eyes swept fondly up and down him, and he saw her swelling tears.

'Bob,' she breathed, 'kiss your mother! You haven't kissed me, Bob, since the day you went away to the academy – nine years ago. And I think –' Her |clear voice shuddered. 'I'm afraid, Bob, that we shall never be together again!'

He kissed her. A sudden cruel tension had closed on his chest. Her troubled loveliness swam in his tears.

'My beautiful, beautiful mother!' he whispered. He drew back to look at her, with a puzzled unease. 'But you didn't want to destroy the comet,' he said quickly. 'I thought you weren't afraid, even – to die.'

'That?' She shrugged away the penalty of her secret. 'But I wish – I almost wish that Commander Kalam had landed half a minute later. Because I'm still afraid your father is right.'

'Why?'

She stood silent for a moment, fear cold on her face.

'Jay will tell you about the man we call Merrin,' she said huskily. 'I saw him only once. That was after he became the prisoner of the Legion. He was shackled and well guarded. Yet, somehow, he was terrible.'

She stood staring toward the jade-and-silver wall, her eyes fixed and sombre as if her mind were seeing something more disturbing.

'He was a giant, Bob.' Dread still trembled in her voice. 'There was a kind of splendour in him, and a terrible strength. He was a helpless captive, yet his face was shining with an unconquered power. He seemed like – well, something more than just a human being.'

She caught Bob's arm, her strong hand quivering.

'He seemed superhuman – immortal and almost invinc-

35

ible and entirely contemptuous of mankind. His mind must be as powerful as his magnificent body – but his emotions can't be quite human. You have to admire him, But you must fear him, too. I don't quite know why, because there certainly isn't much harm left that he can do.

'He didn't speak to me, Bob. He simply turned for an instant to look at me, as they were leading him across to his cell – taking mincing little steps, because of the leg irons. His blue eyes were burning – and they were cold as ice. They were undefeated, carelessly unafraid.

'He laughed at me, as he went on, from a distance I could never reach across. Something in him hadn't been beaten – and never will be! You must guard him well, Bob. For in him you are guarding the lives and the happiness of all your honest fellow men!'

Astonished and puzzled, he whispered, 'I will.'

'Come, Bob,' Jay Kalam was saying. 'It's time to go.'

He embraced his mother.

'I love you, Bob,' she was breathing. 'And I'm – oh! so afraid!' Her slight straight body was trembling against him. 'Be careful, son. Don't let the man called Merrin get away!'

'Good-bye, Robert.' His father shook his hand, speaking with an unaccustomed tremor of emotion in his voice. 'Whatever happens, don't ever forget that you are now an officer on duty with the Legion of Space.'

'Yes, sir.' Bob Star wondered about that unspoken question he had seen in his father's troubled eyes, and he tried hard to answer it. 'I won't forget!'

He went out of the Jade Room with Commander Kalam, and paused abruptly when he saw Giles Habibula, sitting half-asleep on a seat in the wide corridor outside.

'My bodyguards?' he asked quickly. 'Are they coming?'

The commander's dark face warmed, as if to the glow of old memories.

'Giles and Hal?' He nodded quickly. 'They're good men – we served together, you know, long ago. Bring them on aboard.'

A concealed door behind the chart room of the *Invincible* opened into a long chamber that Bob Star was surprised to find upon a warship of space. Golden light from hidden sources fell upon the rich sheen of heavy rugs. The pale ivory walls were hung with exquisite Titanium tapestries. The massive furnishings, in silver-and-black, were luxuriously simple. The long bookshelves and the optiphone, with its tall cabinets of the recorded music and drama of several planets, revealed the scholarly aesthete in the master of the room.

The *Invincible* was now driving outward from the sun, away from yellow-red Mars and the greenish fleck of Phobos. Her humming geodynes – electromagnetic geodesic deflectors, in the language of the engineers – acted to deflect every atom of ship, load, and crew very slightly from the coordinates of the familiar continuum of the four dimensions, so that the vessel was driven around space-time, rather than through it, by a direct reaction against the warp of space itself.

In that hidden room, however, even the vibrant droning of the geodynes was shut away, as if they ran in another space. Nothing gave any faintest sense of the ship's tremendous acceleration and velocity. The crispness of the cooled artificial air suggested springtime in the woods of far-off Earth.

'Sit down, Bob.' Jay Kalam nodded at a great chair, but Bob Star felt too tense and breathless to sit. 'I'm going to tell you about the prisoner we call Merrin, and the unfortunate circumstances that place this grave duty upon you.'

'This man –' Bob Star was trying to seem calm, but his dry voice trembled and sank. 'This man you call Merrin – is he – is he Stephen Orco?'

A shadow of troubled amazement crossed the commander's lean face.

'That is a high secret of the Legion.' His low voice was taut and his dark eyes searching. 'A secret you had no right to know, before today. How did you find out?'

'My mother described the prisoner, back there in the Jade Room,' Bob Star said. 'I knew Stephen Orco, and knew there couldn't be another like him. But I thought –' His voice caught, and his troubled fingers came absently up to that pale, triangular scar on his forehead. 'I thought he was dead.'

'I'm glad that's how you knew.' The commander seemed to relax. 'Because Stephen Orco is dead – and buried – to all except a trusted few.' His face turned grave again. 'When did you know him?'

'Nine years ago.' Bob Star's voice was hoarse with emotion. 'On Earth, at the academy. He was in the graduating section, during my first term. He was handsome, brilliant. At first I was attracted to him. But then –'

He broke off abruptly, his face pale and hard.

'What happened, Bob?' Jay Kalam's tone was warm with a puzzled sympathy. 'Did you quarrel?'

'It was our affair.' Bob Star nodded bleakly. 'For years I meant to find him, as soon as I graduated, and – settle it. But then he showed the Legion what sort he is, with the Jovian Revolt. And I thought he got death for his treason.' He peered at the tall commander. 'Wasn't that the sentence?'

'It's what the public records show,' the commander said quietly. 'But you must tell me about you and Stephen Orco.'

'I can't!' A sort of panic shook Bob Star. 'I haven't told anyone – not even my own parents.'

'I need to know,' Jay Kalam insisted softly. 'Because your singular duty now must be a consequence of that incident – whatever it was.'

Bob Star stood looking for a moment at Jay Kalam, his face hard with a long-remembered bitterness. He nodded soberly.

'You know the tradition of hazing at the academy?'

'The officers have always tolerated it,' Jay Kalam said. 'It is believed to be good for discipline.'

'Maybe it is – usually.' Bob Star shrugged impatiently,

as if to shake off the burden of that old bitterness. 'Anyhow, you know the rule that each new cadet must accept and obey one command from each man in the graduating section?'

The commander nodded quietly.

'I suppose it isn't bad, usually,' Bob Star went on. 'The graduates are learning to be officers, and the new boys learning discipline. The commands are commonly harmless, and I suppose the custom usually makes for comradeship as well as discipline."

A cruel emotion quivered in his voice.

'But Stephen Orco was no usual student. A giant of a man. He was remarkably good-looking, and a great athlete. His hair was red as flame. His eyes were peculiar – a bright, cold blue, and always shining with a clever malice. The instructors used to say he was the most brilliant cadet ever at the academy."

Bob Star's narrowed eyes were staring past Jay Kalam at the dark-hued patterns of a priceless Titanian hanging. In the pain of that old injury, he had forgotten his first awe of the tall commander. His words fell swiftly, hard as slivers of ice.

'Stephen Orco had no real friends, I think. All the boys must have been secretly afraid of him. Yet he did have a kind of popularity. His remarkable strength and his malicious wit made it uncomfortable to be his enemy. More than that, he had a kind of evil fascination.

'He was a born leader. His reckless audacity matched his uncommon abilities. He could dare anything. And he had a pride to match his capacities. It made him try to excel in everything – usually with success. It seemed to me that he had a jealous enmity toward every possible rival. He loved no one. He was completely selfish in every friendship.

'From the first day, he hated me.'

The commander looked faintly startled, beneath his grave reserve.

'Do you know why?'

39

'Jealousy, I suppose,' Bob Star said. 'He knew I was John Star's heir. He assumed that I would be chosen to take my mother's place as keeper of the peace.' He shook his head. 'There couldn't have been any other reason.'

'Did he mistreat you?'

'From the first day.' Bob Star's nervous fingers traced that scar again. 'He injured me in every way he could. He tried to keep me from winning any honours – perhaps he wanted to keep me from qualifying to be keeper. He did his best to turn all the instructors and the other students against me. He used me for the butt of his cruel practical jokes. He made things pretty rough for me, until he graduated.'

He paused unhappily, biting his quivering lip.

'I've tried to forget what he did to me,' he whispered. 'But there was one thing –'

'Yes?' the commander urged him. 'What was that?'

'It was one night, just before the end of the term,' he went on abruptly, his low voice quick and breathless. 'I was walking alone on the campus – I was worn out from my first final examination in geodesic navigation, and upset because someone had poured ink over all my notes and a finished term paper in my desk – I suppose Stephen Orco was responsible for that, too, though I never really knew.

'Anyhow I met him in the dark, with three of his friends. Or perhaps I shouldn't call them friends – it was fear that held them around him, not affection. They stopped me. Stephen Orco asked me if I had obeyed that customary command from him. I said I hadn't. He turned to the others. They whispered, I heard the others snicker. Then he came came back to me, and gave me his command.'

Bob Star paused, white-faced.

'What was that command?'

'He ordered me to repeat a statement after him. An ugly thing. He wanted me to say that I wasn't John Star's son. He wanted me to say that my father's infamous cousin, Eric the Pretender, had been my mother's lover, and that I was a coward and a weakling, unfit to be the keeper. He wanted me to swear, on my honour as a future officer of the Legion, that his monstrous lie was true.

'Of course I wouldn't.' Bob Star's low voice was hoarse again with that remembered pain. 'One of his friends objected that the hazing tradition gave him no right to go so far, but one glance from Orco was enough to shut him up.

'We were near the academy museum. It was closed and dark, but one of the men had been doing research on the old weapons displayed there, and he had a key. Orco made him open the back door, and they dragged me into the building.

'They took me down into a little basement room, where they wouldn't be interrupted – for I had made friends of my own, in spite of Orco. They did various things to me, but I didn't speak. Stephen Orco's terrible pride was burning cold in his eyes. I think my stubbornness made him angry – if you can imagine that.

'He exhausted the customary penalties, and thought of new ones. He was clever, and he had a taste for such work. Even after his three companions got frightened, he wouldn't agree to let me go.

'Finally, he sent one of the others up to break open a display case and bring him down a rusty torture implement that dated from the last corrupt reigns of the Empire, when the democratic Greens were about to overthrow the power-rotted Purples. A device invented to break political prisoners. It was called the Iron Confessor.'

'Huh?' The commander peered suddenly at that pale scar, with dark, startled eyes. 'I think I remember seeing that display. Isn't the thing a sort of helmet?'

'There's a wide iron ring that goes around the head,' Bob Star said huskily. 'And a sort of three-edged blade that can be forced through a hole in it, as the screws are tightened, into the scalp and the skull of the victim.

'I think Stephen Orco was showing his jealousy, then. He couldn't forget that I came from the old imperial family. If he had been John Star's son – or the Pretender's either – I think he would have been plotting to restore the Empire.

41

Anyhow, he called that torture device the Purple crown, and I could see the savage envy in the way he made me wear it.'

Jay Kalam stood staring at the scar. 'He didn't do – that!'

'He made his men hold me,' Bob Star said. 'He put that ring on my head, and tightened the screws until I felt the blood running down my face. He kept commanding me to repeat that wicked lie. Still I wouldn't do it, and my silence seemed to goad him.

'The Iron Confessor was more than the ring and the blade. There was another part, that had been smashed before it was put in the museum. Orco repaired that, while his men held me there with that blade in my skull. I don't know exactly what it was, or how it worked – I didn't have much attention left, just then, for mechanical details. But Orco said it used supersonic vibration, tuned to stimulate the pain centres of the brain. It looked like a radio amplifier. A cable ran from it to that three edged blade. What it did was to transform a voice into sensations of intolerable pain.

'Stephen Orco stood in front of me, when he got it hooked up. The room was dark, but I could see his face in the glow from the tubes of that device. The hair red like flame. The blue eyes triumphant and mocking and terrible. He began talking into a little microphone, and that thing turned his voice into great waves of red agony beating at my mind.

'It felt unendurable. But I was already exhausted from trying to get away. The others were all grown men, and trained athletes. I was twelve years old, growing weak from loss of blood, and already half unconscious with pain. There was nothing I could do.

'Orco kept on talking, gradually twisting the dials of that fiendish device to step up the intensity of agony. The Iron Confessor had been invented by my own family, he said, to extract confessions from enemies. It was guaranteed, he said, to make anybody confess anything.

'He said it was based on the secret principles of political conversion first discovered by a party called the Reds, a thousand years ago. The tuned ultrasonic vibrations from that blade could destroy the synaptic patterns of my brain, he said – to break my will and make the truth of everything he told me.

'And I was terribly afraid for a while – afraid of yielding to him. But suddenly, even with that knife in my skull and his voice burning like a flame into my brain, I felt that I was strong enough. I felt that nothing he could do would beat me. I looked up at him, and told him to do his worst and promised to kill him whenever I got the chance.

'That seemed to heighten his anger. He stepped up the pain of that vibration again, and he said he was going to fix me so that I'd be afraid to kill anybody. Then he repeated that wicked lie, and kept commanding me to swear that it was true.

' "Say it, pup!" he would shout at me, his voice trembling with his own fury and transformed to pure agony flaming out from that blade in my skull. Then he would turn up the amplifier. And then he would shout again, "Say it, pup!"

'I didn't say it – not at least so long as I was conscious. But I'm not sure what really happened, toward the end. It was a kind of nightmare. That dark room, and his face proud and angry and dreadful in that faint glow of light, and his voice hammering at my mind with red agony.

' "Say it, pup!"

'I knew at the end that my will was weaker than that machine. And I must have finally given in – I'm afraid I did.' Bob Star stood shuddering for a moment, his thin hands clenched. 'I don't know what happened,' he repeated huskily. 'But it's hard to imagine that Stephen Orco gave up before I spoke.

'The next thing I really knew, I was in bed in the infirmary, with my head bandaged and a nurse giving me a shot of something to quiet my nerves. She told me that Stephen Orco and his friends had brought me there about dawn.

Their story was that they had found me wandering on the beach, under the cliffs, with my head slashed open.

'I told everybody that I had fallen in the dark, and hurt myself accidentally.'

'Why did you do that?' Jay Kalam shook his head, in puzzled reproof. 'Why didn't you report the truth? Stephen Orco would have been punished and discharged from the Legion – he would never have had the opportunity to lead the Jovian Revolt.'

'It was our quarrel,' Bob Star whispered hoarsely. 'Ever since those vibrations of pain were burning into my brain, I've meant to kill him, if I could.' He shook his head and muttered again, uncertainly, '– if I could.'

'How's that?' The commander gave him a long, troubled look. 'Assuming that it became your duty to kill Stephen Orco, and that you had the means at hand, couldn't you do it?'

'I don't quite know.' Bob Star shivered again. 'I can't remember what happened at last, or whether I really gave up. He kept promising to break me, so that I could never kill anybody. I'm afraid – afraid he did. Because I think my brain was damaged by that ultrasonic vibration – if that was what it was. There's still a pain throbbing in my head. A little hammer of red agony, pounding day and night. In nine years, it hasn't stopped.'

Bob Star's face was white, and sweat had broken out on his forehead.

'I wasn't a coward – before that night,' he whispered hoarsely. 'I wasn't the weakling he wanted to make me.' He sank abruptly into the big chair, looking miserably up at Jay Kalam. 'But now, commander – I don't know.'

Chapter Five

THE HONOUR OF THE LEGION

The tall commander of the Legion stood for a time scraping thoughtfully with one lean finger at the lean angle of his jaw, studying Bob Star.

'I'm glad you've told me this,' he said at last, his voice quiet and very grave. 'I understand the way you feel, because once I thought it would be impossible for me to kill a man.' His dark eyes closed for a moment, and his face drew stern as if with some memory of pain. 'But sometimes it must be done. I learned that long ago, and found that I could do it.'

He stepped abruptly forward.

'And so must you, Bob. You can – and must! As things stand now, it is very likely to become your duty to take the life of Stephen Orco.'

Those softly spoken words brought Bob Star out of his chair.

'How is that, commander?' He was trembling, and he had to gasp for his breath. 'I'd give anything for the chance!' Something checked his eager voice, and something made him bite his lip. 'But I'm afraid – afraid I couldn't do it.'

Chimes rang softly, then. A massive door swung open, to admit once more the deep-toned, vibrant song of the geo-dynes that drove the battleship. A steward came in, pushing a little wheeled table. He saluted.

'Breakfast, commander,' he announced. 'For two.'

Jay Kalam motioned silently for him to go. The heavy door closed behind him, and once more it seemed that the long, ivory-walled room was somewhere far from the racing ship.

'Why might it be my special duty to kill Stephen Orco?'

Bob Star was whispering. 'And how does it happen that he's still alive, now so long after his execution was announced?'

'A strange affair.' Jay Kalam stood frowning gravely, ignoring the covered table the steward had left. 'An unfortunate aftermath of the Jovian Revolt. The full history of that rebellion has never been made public, but I must outline it to you now – so that you will understand the peculiar status of Stephen Orco, and the supreme importance of your present duty.'

Bob Star nodded, listening breathlessly.

'Orco himself is a sinister riddle, from the very beginning,' the commander went on gravely. 'Many people besides yourself have found him queerly inhuman. Perhaps he is. Our investigators have been at work ever since he turned traitor, and still they have discovered nothing whatever about his origin.'

'But I remember his parents,' Bob Star broke in. 'They visited the academy, not long before – that night.' He found his fingers on that scar again, and dropped them self-consciously. 'He gave a party for them. He made a point of inviting all my friends, and leaving me out.'

'They were only foster-parents,' Jay Kalam said. 'His adoptive father, Edwin Orco, seems to have found him, when he was just an infant, under peculiar circumstances. Orco was a wealthy planter. He had extensive holdings through the asteroids. His home was on Pallas. Our investigators learned what we know about the finding of Stephen Orco, from his old servants.

"It happened nearly thirty years ago. Orco was cruising in towards Mars in his space yacht. He and his wife had been visiting some of their properties scattered through the smaller asteroids, and they were coming to Mars for the social season. Their route had taken them far off the usual space lanes.

'Some forty million miles off Mars, their navigator discovered an unusual object, adrift in space. It had tripped the meteor-detectors, but it was obviously no common meteorite. The navigator's report aroused Orco's curiosity enough so that he turned back to examine the object.

'It proved to be a cylinder of magnelithium alloy, eight feet long. It had a carefully machined screw cap, which was sealed at several points with masses of black wax. Impressed upon each seal, in scarlet was a curious symbol: the looped cross – the *crux ansata*, which is an ancient symbol of life – above crossed bones.

'Orco had gone out in a space suit to examine the object. He decided to bring it aboard, through the air-locks, and open it. His wife objected. The crossed bones, she insisted, meant danger. The shape and dimensions of the object rather suggested a coffin, and she suggested that it might contain a corpse, dead of some dreadful contagion.

'But Edwin Orco was a hardy man. It was not timidity that had won his fortune, out on that high frontier. And his curiosity must have been burning. In the end, he had the cylinder dragged into the air-lock. Then, when no member of his crew proved willing to touch it, he shut himself into the chamber with it. He broke the seals, and unscrewed the cap.

'The walls of the cylinder were heavy, and carefully insulated. Inside, it was fitted with tanks of oxygen, water, and liquid food. There were heaters and thermostats and condensers to dry the air. In brief, except for lack of power, the thing was a miniature space ship.

'In the midst of the apparatus, in a kind of cradle, lay Stephen Orco. A red-haired tot, not a year old. He was naked, and there was nothing to identify him. Apparently he was never able to tell anything of his past history. Edwin Orco advertised discreetly for information, offering large rewards, but nothing was ever forthcoming.

'Stephen Orco must have had, as you say, some unusual fascination. One glimpse of the child's wide blue eyes won Edwin Orco's childless wife. The couple adopted the infant. They gave it every advantage their wealth could buy, even to securing the appointment to the academy.'

'His own brilliance would have been enough to win him

that,' Bob Star put in. 'He could have had any scholarship he wanted.'

'Anyhow,' Jay Kalam went on, 'he graduated with top honours. He went into service, and got the rapid promotions that his abilities seemed to earn. Within four years, he had his own ship. Not two years later he was placed in command of the Jupiter Patrol.

'The Jovian satellites, I suppose you know, were settled largely by exiled Purples – enemies of the democratic Green Hall. They were moved there when the Empire was overthrown, two centuries ago.'

'I know,' Bob Star agreed. 'My own grandfather was born on Callisto.'

'Within a year after he assumed command of the Jupiter Patrol,' the commander continued, 'we began to receive ultrawave dispatches from Stephen Orco, reporting an unexpected uprising of the Purples. He stated that he had the situation well in hand, however, and asked for no reinforcements.

'For several weeks we did nothing – until a band of fugitives reached Ceres in a space-yacht, with the information that Stephen Orco was himself the guiding spirit of the revolt, and that the fighting had begun when his conspirators attacked men in the Patrol. Civilian friends of the Green Hall were being systematically murdered.

'I recalled every possible Legion ship to the Martian yards, from as far away as Mercury and Contra-Saturn –'

'I remember when we heard about it, in the classrooms at the academy,' Bob Star put in. 'I hadn't seen Stephen Orco, since the time they tortured me. I tried to get into the fleet, to even that old score, but my request for duty was never approved.'

'Your father asked me to ignore it,' Jay Kalam said. 'I didn't know what you have just told me – or you might have had a chance to get your man. Because that was the most serious crisis the Legion has faced since Eric the Pretender brought those monstrous invaders back from the Runaway Star to help him restore the Empire.

'As soon as the fleet was gathered in the Martian yards, I took your mother aboard the flagship. From the reports coming back from Jupiter, I was already sure we were going to need her weapon.

'Our outward flight was not opposed. We approached Callisto without meeting any hostile action, and I dispatched an ultrawave message calling on the mutineers to surrender. The answer was something like a sun, fired at us from the fortress above the city of Lel.'

'The sun-gun?' Bob Star whispered. 'I heard rumours, you know, in spite of the censorship and the way my father tried to shield me.'

'The correspondents named it that,' Jay Kalam nodded. 'The weapon was an improvement over something the monsters of the Runaway Star had used against us twenty years before. An energy vortex, which warps the coordinates of time and space to make all the heavy elements as unstable as plutonium – and creates a resistless attraction to draw more matter into its terrible whirlpool of atomic annihilation.'

His dark face had stiffened.

'Stephen Orco must be as brilliant as you say. He had designed that dreadful thing from scraps of information the exiles of Callisto had got from the creatures of the Runaway Star, while the Purples under Eric were in alliance with them. But somehow he had multiplied the range and power of it. That first shot destroyed two of our finest ships. I saw at once that Orco's weapon could reach every planet in the System, with those atomic shots.

'Your mother had already assembled her own secret weapon. As much as I dislike wholesale destruction, I asked her to wipe out the city of Lel with all its surrounding fortifications.

'You saw the instrument of the peace, Bob, back there in the Jade Room. Your mother must have told you that the working of it is not spectacular. I was not surprised that nothing seemed to happen when she tried to operate it. But I could see her expression of puzzled fear when she turned to me, a moment afterwards.

' "It doesn't work," she whispered.

'One glance at the screen of a tele-periscope was enough to show that the fortifications of Lel were still unchanged. I was able to step up the magnification enough to see the atomic gun itself – a colossal skeleton tube of metal girders, set up on a mountaintop beside the city.

'While I was looking, another vortex came spinning toward us. A sort of spiral nebula in miniature, in which meteors and ships exploded as furiously as if they had suddenly turned to pure plutonium. That second shot caught three more cruisers, and your mother saw at once that we had been defeated.

'Someone else, she told me, had come upon the principle of AKKA. She tried to explain, without compromising her secret, that the weapon utilizes a singular instability of the universe which is such that any master of the device can prevent its use by any other.'

Bob Star was nodding.

'She spoke to me about what she called a fulcrum,' he said. 'The device she puts together is a lever, and the mind supplies the force, but there is only one fulcrum. His breath caught sharply. 'Had Stephen Orco discovered – that?'

The commander nodded bleakly.

'Your mother's failure was sufficient evidence, she said, that another master of AKKA was fighting us. Her weapon wouldn't work again, she told me, until that other person was dead – or at least until his instrument had been taken from him.'

'Of course your mother was able to keep Orco from using the secret against us, but his atomic gun itself was enough to beat our fleet. We lost six more vessels as we fled. A triumphant ultrawave message from Orco followed us.

'His message was insolently phrased. It confirmed your mother's belief that he was the new master of AKKA. It demanded that the Green Hall recognize him as the supreme ruler of an independent Jovian Empire.

'But even that wasn't enough to satisfy Orco's imperial ambition. He demanded trading rights and other concessions on every planet, and humiliating limitations upon the strength and movements of the Legion. It was clear that he planned to dominate the whole System.'

Jay Kalam stood rigidly straight amid the rich simplicity of that great, soundless room upon the racing battleship. His lean face was grimly set. His dark eyes were narrowed sternly. The vibrant ring of his low voice seemed to Bob Star like an undying echo of mighty deeds.

'We were defeated,' he said softly. 'But not vanquished. The Legion has never been vanquished, Bob. You must remember that.'

'Yes, sir.' Instinctively, Bob Star stood straighter.

'While the politicians on the Council stalled for time and debated how to answer Orco's ultimatum, we set out to build our own atomic gun. We had our spectrographic observations of those hurled suns, and a few hints your father found in the Pretender's private papers, in the library of the Purple Hall.

'That information was incomplete and some of it inaccurate. But your father made a brilliant guess about how the deformation of space-time increases nuclear instability. I did what I was able. It was your mother – aided, perhaps, by her own secret science – who showed us how to control the movement and growth of the field of instability.

'We built, and set up on Ceres, an atomic gun fully equal to the one on Callisto. Stephen Orco had been organizing his new empire and dispatching his ultimatums without much haste, because he thought we were completely at his mercy. The successful erection of our atomic gun on Ceres was a surprise that defeated him.

'Neither weapon could destroy the other, for the control fields of each could deflect approaching shots. Stephen Orco's weapon was powerful enough, given time, to desolate every planet in the entire system – one shot from Callisto reduced ten thousand square miles of Mercury to smoking radioactive lava.

51

'But our weapon was equally effective. It was a simpler task to blot life from the moons of Jupiter than from the rest of the System. We should have finished first. And Stephen Orco, as you say, is a remarkably brilliant man. He saw at once that he was defeated. He was too intelligent to carry on a clearly hopeless battle. He immediately offered to surrender, when our first vortex struck Callisto.

'He demanded, however, that we guarantee his life. He required the personal word of every member of the Green Hall, and of myself, for the Legion, that we would protect his life at every cost. He made an odd exception, however, with regard to you, Bob – until today, I didn't understand why.'

Bob Star leaned forward, to ask hoarsely. 'What was that?'

'I think I recall his words,' said Jay Kalam. 'Here's what he said:

' "Leave out Robert Star. He and I already have an engagement regarding my life. If that young pup has the guts to kill me, let him do it." '

That challenge jerked Bob Star forward. He was trembling. His thin face tightened, and his nails dug into his palms. The triangular scar on his forehead turned white.

'He needs killing,' he whispered harshly. 'But I'm afraid – afraid I couldn't do it.' His mouth had fallen a little open, and he stood mopping at the sweat on his pale face. 'I can't remember all that happened, but I know the Iron Confessor did something to my brain. Orco said he was going to break me. And I'm afraid – afraid –'

'So am I.' The commander smiled bleakly. 'But we are soldiers of the Legion.' For a moment he was silent, his dark face stern and grave. 'The word of an officer of the Legion has seldom been broken, except by a few such men as the Pretender and Orco himself. Mine will not be broken. I am not going to kill Stephen Orco.'

His sombre eyes dwelt upon Bob Star.

'But since he made that mocking exception in your case, Bob, it may become necessary for us to take advantage of it. Understand, I'm not commanding you to kill him. What I'm going to do is to leave you at his prison, with an independent authority to take whatever action you see fit. Your orders will be simply not to let Stephen Orco escape.'

'Yes, commander.' Bob Star wet his lips. 'I – I understand.'

'It's unfortunate that we had to spare the traitor's life.' Jay Kalam frowned regretfully. 'Your father was opposed to that concession. I urged the Council to agree to it, however, because it might have cost billions of lives to carry on the war long enough to kill him.

'Perhaps it seems surprising that Orco was willing to trust the Legion, but he evidently knows our standards of honour – even though he chose to disregard them, in his own career. The terms were settled, anyhow, and he became our prisoner – no doubt the most dangerous man that locks ever held.'

'He must be.' Bob Star stepped quickly backward. 'If he knows my mother's secret!'

'He has been well guarded,' Jay Kalam continued. 'We announced that he had been condemned and executed – to discourage the efforts of possible rescuers. In a secret place, we built the strongest fortress that our engineers could devise. He is held there, under the name of Merrin, dead to the world outside.

'But not,' the commander added quietly, 'to the Cometeers.'

'Eh?' Bob Star felt stiff with dismay. 'How's that?'

'The creatures of the cometary object have discovered that Stephen Orco is alive,' Jay Kalam said soberly. 'That's the reason your father was so set upon the immediate destruction of the comet.'

'How – ' Bob Star gulped to find his voice. 'How did they find out?'

'Certain information about Stephen Orco, including the location of his prison, was kept in a vault in the Green Hall. The vault was believed to be impregnable, and it was always guarded by trusted men.

53

'But the invisible beings from the comet slipped into the building. They killed four guards – with some unknown agency. They picked locks that Giles Habibula himself had tested and failed to open. They carried off the documents relating to Stephen Orco.'

'If they should set him free –' Bob Star shook his head, apprehension grey on his face. 'I don't like to think of that. Stephen Orco has no loyalty to mankind. If the Cometeers are going to be our enemies, he would gladly join them.'

'It's hard to believe that, of any human being.' The commander lifted his head, smiling gravely. 'Anyhow, I still hope to find that the Cometeers intend to be our friends. If they fail to reciprocate our gesture of friendship, remember your duty.' His voice rang hard. 'Don't let Orco escape!'

Bob Star sank back into the big chair, shuddering. His thin face was a mask of agony, and the scar of the Iron Confessor was lividly white. His tortured eyes stared up at Jay Kalam, mutely pleading.

'I'll try,' he whispered miserably. 'But I'm – afraid!'

Chapter Six

THE GIRL IN THE WALL

The *Invincible* drove down toward the south pole of Neptune. The eighth planet was a vast and inhospitable world of pale twilight and bitter night. The enormous installations of the planetary engineers, running through long centuries, had finally cleared the poisonous methane and ammonia from the air, generated enough free oxygen to support human life, and raised the surface temperature many degrees. There were cities over the rich mines in the equatorial regions, but the immense polar continent was not yet ready for colonization. A frozen wilderness larger than all Earth, blanketed with freezing, everlasting fogs, it was marked on the interplanetary charts:

Uninhabited and dangerous; shipping keep clear.

In disregard of that warning, the *Invincible* landed three degrees from the pole. Bob Star and his two bodyguards came down a ramp, to a dark frozen plain. Already shivering, they ran away from the ship. Rockets thundered behind them. They dropped flat to escape the sudden hot hurricane of the jets. The ship lifted and vanished in the cloudy, greenish twilight, carrying Jay Kalam forward on his mission to test the good will of the Cometeers.

A squad of Legionnaires came out of the foggy dark. They challenged the three, examined their credentials, and guided them to a fortress standing on a low and barren hill. They were almost upon it before Bob Star could see anything. Abruptly, then, a vast and massive wall loomed out of the greenish gloom.

'The wall is ring-shaped, sir,' the guard officer informed him, with an awed respect for Jay Kalam's signature upon his papers. 'There's a circular field inside, where our four cruisers are lying now. But you don't see the real prison at all. It's a buried cylinder of perdurite. Merrin's cell is a thousand feet below the field.'

A ponderous, armoured door admitted them to the hundred-foot thickness of the wall. Bob Star asked immediately to see the prisoner. And at last, beyond confusing, narrow passages walled with grey perdurite, behind huge cylindrical doors that were elaborately locked, beyond hidden elevators and grimly alert guards in turrets of vitrilith, he looked upon the man he must kill.

A huge door let him into a small square room, where two sentries watched. Its farther wall was a thick, shining sheet of vitrilith. Beyond that impregnable transparency was Stephen Orco's cell.

The prisoner sat in a big chair, reading. He held a glass of some red drink in one great hand, and his splendid body looked relaxed in a green dressing gown. Bob Star could see the angle of his handsome face, and the light smile clinging to his wide, womanish mouth.

'This is Merrin, sir,' the officer said. 'He was sealed beyond that vitrilith wall when the prison was completed, two years ago. No one has talked to him since. The cell is soundproof, and the guards are ordered to ignore any sort of signal he may attempt. All metal objects are kept from him. Air, water, and liquid foods are pumped to him through screened tubes from another room accessible only to the commanding officer –'

He broke off to indicate a small red button on the grey wall beside him.

'I must warn you, sir. Don't touch that button. It is connected to a valve that would fill the cell with a lethal gas. Our orders, however, are to preserve the prisoner's life as a trust of the Legion.'

Bob Star scarcely heard the man's last words, above the sudden ringing in his ears. Abrupt sweat chilled him. He swayed with a sick faintness. The little red disc stared at him, like a sinister eye.

He had to touch it – that was all.

And the score of nine years would be settled. An intolerable burden would be lifted from him. Even that old pain, he felt, would somehow have to stop throbbing in his head. His haunting fear would go, and the System would be safe from the malign genius of Stephen Orco –

He was aware, then, that the prisoner had seen him. The blue eyes, cold and burning with a reckless defiance, had lifted from the book. The handsome face smiled mockingly. Stephen Orco got lazily to his feet and came strolling to that transparent, unbreakable wall. He pointed at the red button, and slapped his leg with silent merriment. His full lips formed a derisive, soundless greeting.

Bob Star felt a sudden desire to speak to him. This was their first meeting since that night of torture. He tried to hope that his haunting fear would somehow vanish, an illusion born of pain, when he met Stephen Orco under these new circumstances.

Yes, the officer said, there was a telephone, but its use was forbidden.

'You saw my orders,' Bob Star insisted. 'It's necessary for me to speak with Merrin.'

After a conference with the commandant, it was arranged. Bob Star was left alone in the square, grey room outside that crystal wall. A magnetic speaker thumped and then he heard the clear, rich baritone of Stephen Orco:

'Greetings, Bob! I'm amused at your efforts to touch that red button.'

Bob Star felt his face stiffen.

'Laugh if you like,' he muttered harshly. 'But I can do it – if I must.'

'Try again, if you like.' Orco's taunting laughter rang loud from the speaker. 'No, you'll never do it, Bob. Not since that night with the Iron Confessor – I've seen too many times what that ultrasonic pulse does to brain tissue and the thing called courage. I've never been afraid that you would kill me. And I'm certain no other will – because of a foolish code the Legion has.'

Shuddering with a sick humiliation, Bob Star swung

desperately toward that red button. He reached for it grimly – but his old fear yelled, *you can't!* A numbing chill struck down his hand. He staggered back, his shoulders sagging with defeat. Tears blurred his eyes. His hands knotted impotently.

'I'm really glad to see you,' Stephen Orco's voice was booming. 'Because you must have been sent here upon the foolish hope that you could destroy me. That means that my already rather fantastic defences are considered inadequate. I conclude therefore that I have powerful allies outside, and that I may hope shortly to be set free.'

'Not if I can prevent it!'

'But you can't, Bob. I've beaten you.' Bob Star was astonished and disturbed to see the black enormity of hate that peered suddenly through that mocking levity. 'I've broken you, for ever.'

Orco's voice was suddenly lower, a breathless, thickened rasping, monstrous and clotted with his hate.

'When I first learned of your existence, while I was only a child, it filled me with fury to think that an utterly incompetent weakling, through no effort or merit of his own, should one day become the most powerful of men – while I had nothing. I resolved then, before I had ever seen the gilded boy of the Purple Hall, to crush you and take all your heritage for myself.'

Stephen Orco paused. His wide mouth broke into a sudden, brilliant smile of satisfaction, and his tone was light again when he resumed: 'You weren't hard to break, Bob. The Iron Confessor killed all the danger in you, that first night. Afterwards, I admit, ethical questions disturbed me, but time soon answered them. Consider it this way: One of us has AKKA given to him; the other must discover it by his own efforts. Which better deserves it?'

'The keeping of AKKA isn't any sort of selfish advantage,' Bob Star answered huskily. 'It is a tremendous task, that fills the life and finally demands the death of the keeper.' He caught his breath. 'But how – how did you discover it?'

The prisoner smiled patronizingly.

'I'm going to tell you, Bob,' he said blandly. 'If only to establish my superior rights to the secret and the perfect justice of my actions. I might remark, by the way, that I don't intend to let the care of the secret become any sort of distressing moral burden to me. The trouble with you, Bob, is just that you weren't big enough for the job.'

He shook his head mockingly, at Bob Star's trembling impotence.

'Anyhow,' he continued easily, 'I simply followed the methods of investigation that should have suggested themselves to any person of intelligence. I collected the data available, formulated hypotheses by experiment, and so finally arrived at a satisfactory conclusion.

'While I was still at the academy, I obtained secret access to a secret library, and studied there all the existing accounts of the use of AKKA, since the time of its discovery by your mother's great ancestor, Charles Anthar – while he himself was a prisoner, guarded almost as carefully as I am.

'The last recorded use of the weapon had been to destroy Earth's old satellite – after it had been seized and fortified by the Pretender's unsuspecting allies. With my foster father's space yacht, I searched the orbit the satellite had followed. I finally found three small metallic buttons.

'No larger than the end of my thumb, they were all that remained of the Moon. I have since come to realize how very fortunate I was to find a single atom. It was only because your mother was working hastily, with a crudely improvised instrument, that the annihilation of the heavy elements was not quite complete.

'Some months of careful work, in a laboratory financed from my foster father's funds, revealed the nature of the partial effect of AKKA upon those metallic specimens. From effect to cause was a matter of mathematical reasoning. It remained but to test alternative hypotheses, and elaborate the surviving construction – and the secret was mine.'

The prisoner paused, smiling again.

'Don't you agree with me, Bob, that such abilities merit

reward? I am certainly the most gifted of men; reason assures me that I am therefore their rightful ruler. And I should have been that already, Bob – but for one blunder.'

Hoarsely, Bob Star whispered. 'What was that?'

'I failed to kill your mother.' Stephen Orco shrugged carelessly. 'The trouble was that I didn't see, until too late, the singular limitation of the weapon. I didn't try to use it until she was also trying. It failed for both of us, and that blunder put me here. But it's one I sha'n't repeat, when I find another chance'

He chuckled maliciously.

'I'm not afraid to tell you that,' he added cheerfully. 'Because I know you can't touch that red button – not even to save your mother's life.'

Bob Star knew then what he must do, but still he couldn't do it – at any rate, not yet. Wearily, he signalled for the guards and had the telephone disconnected. With the prisoner sealed again in the tomb of silence, he waited alone in the little outer room, bleakly resolved to stay there until he could press that button – or until the need was gone.

Stephen Orco had calmly returned to his chair and his book. He relaxed in the green robe, sipping at his drink, apparently oblivious to any danger to his life. Twice again Bob Star left the hard bench where he waited, trying to touch that button.

The simple act was utterly impossible. The effort did nothing but accelerate that unceasing throb of pain inside his head and turn him faint with illness. He gave up for the time, desperately hopeful that the stimulus of emergency would nerve him for the deed, if any crisis came.

Hopelessly, he stumbled back to the bench.

His eyes, as he sat there, widened abruptly. His breath sucked in, and his lean hands clenched. He leaned forward, staring at the hard grey wall. For he thought that its surface had begun to shimmer with vague, moving shadows.

The massive door was still locked behind him. The alarm gongs were silent. The sheet of vitrilith was still intact, and that lounging giant beyond it still ignored him. There was no hint of another presence with him – none save the creeping shadows on the wall. He watched them, breath-taken.

A misty blue circle flickered against the grey. Ghostly shadow shapes darted through it. Abruptly then, as if some tri-dimensional projector had come suddenly into focus, the hard armour of the wall melted into an amazing scene.

He looked into a curious chamber, sunk now like a deep niche into the cell wall. Its surface followed tapering spiral curves, and the colour of it was an absolute black, spangled with small crystals of brilliant blue that were various as snowflakes.

The girl stood inside that sudden hollow in the wall, upon a many-angled pedestal of blue transparency. An unsteady flame burned deep within that great sapphire block, and its fitful light danced against the tiny flakes of blue.

Vividly real against that spiral shell of darkness and blue fire, the girl stood watching him. Her expression had a desperate, almost agonized intentness. One slim white arm was thrust out and upward, in what seemed a gesture of warning. The pale oval of her face was grave with the expectation of danger, and her bright lips parted, as he watched, as if she had spoken some warning word.

No sound reached him, however, and the silence brought him a sudden doubt of what he saw. With a bewildered shrug, he got up from the bench and started uncertainly toward the wall. Her solemn brown eyes followed his movement, in a way that made him sure that she was really watching, and she stopped him with an imperative gesture.

She turned, then, to point through the transparent slab at Stephen Orco, who now seemed absorbed in his book and drink. Keeping her distressed golden eyes on Bob Star, she gestured urgently toward the red button that he had failed to touch.

He started toward it again, and again all the agony of the Iron Confessor rose up out of the past to stop him. He turned helplessly back toward the girl, with a sick misery in his eyes. She plainly wanted him to kill Stephen Orco – and he wondered suddenly if her panic-stricken loveliness could be nothing more than hallucination, the vivid symbol of his own impotent desire.

She saw him turn, and a tragic sadness shadowed her face. The light died in her golden eyes. White knuckles lifted to her mouth, in a gesture of bleak frustration. Suddenly then, she started as if she had heard some silent voice. She shuddered, beckoning him toward the red button again, desperately and hopelessly.

Then, as the urgent pleading of her face changed to sad compassion, a bomb of cold flame exploded in the blue pedestal. Sapphire sparks danced across the crystal rime upon the spiral walls. Blue radiance filled the niche, and slowly died. Dark shadows thickened, and silently dissolved.

The grey wall was whole again.

And Bob Star was once more alone. He swayed, trembling. Tears of defeat and despair burned his eyes. He flung his head and looked sharply at Stephen Orco, who was just setting down his empty glass, his attention still lost in the book.

Confusion roared in Bob Star's mind. Had she been real? All his doubts had been suspended, in that last moment of his useless effort and her sad departure, but now the question hammered at him. A living person – where? Or only a tormented projection of his own unendurable predicament.

He jumped, when the gong shattered the silence in the room. Harshly, from a speaker beside it, rasped a hoarse command: 'Emergency stations? Secure all doors! Stand –' The voice choked strangely. 'Quick.' It was a ragged whisper now. 'Invisible things – I can't see –'

Now! Bob Star's breath gasped out. He must act now, or betray the Legion. Fighting a numbing inertia, he swung towards the grey wall. The push button winked at him, a red, malicious eye. He was aware that Stephen Orco had laid aside the book, to watch him with a careless amusement.

He contrived to take another halting step. Abrupt sweat chilled him. His ears were roaring again. For the effort had plunged him back into the grasp of the Iron Confessor.

Once more he felt the pressure of that cold steel band around his head, and the cruel slow thrust of that three-edged blade, and the burning agony of that unendurable vibration. He could see Stephen Orco's furious face against the darkness of that room, and hear his savage voice, amplified and changed to unbearable pain:

'So you don't like it, pup? Then you had better change your mind. Because you'll never be able to do anything about it. I'm fixing you now so you can't kill anybody. This machine is stronger than anybody's will. When it gets through breaking you, you'll stay broken. Even if you weren't a snivelling coward before, you'll be one now.

'You can't kill me. You can't kill –'

Those taunting words echoed again in his mind, with the imperative effect of a post-hypnotic suggestion. He couldn't kill – but he must! The image of that frightened girl in the wall came back to spur him on, and he took another dragging step toward that push button.

But still he couldn't kill—

Something was wrong with the lights in the room. They were turning green. Or was there a green light shining through the massive door behind him? The crisis was here. Now he had to act, and there were only two more steps –

A greenish mist had flooded the room, rising swiftly against the transparent barrier that separated him from Stephen Orco – or was it only in his eyes? The grey walls swam, until he thought they were going to dissolve into another inexplicable vista.

His skin began to prickle strangely. Something numbed all his sensations. Stiffness seized his limbs. He thrust his arm out frantically toward that red push button – or tried to. But he no longer had an arm. Darkness annihilated everything. He didn't know when he hit the floor.

Chapter Seven

THE BEAST OF THE MISTS

The muttered thunder of descending rockets awoke Bob Star. Bitter cold had stiffened his cramped limbs, and his eyes opened upon oppressive green twilight. He found himself sprawled upon frozen ground, still numb with that tingling paralysis which had robbed him of consciousness.

Groping desperately for recollection, he found a disturbing conviction that the gap in his consciousness had contained something unthinkably hideous – something that his mind had sealed away, to preserve its sanity.

After a moment, however, the sickening fact of his own failure came back. Despair swept away that other disquieting half-memory, and he sank back for a time in a crushed and hopeless apathy, until the increasing sound of the rockets became too loud to be ignored. Gasping in a great breath of that icy air, he sat up stiffly.

He was bewildered to find himself at the very brink of an appalling chasm. The flat and barren face of Neptune broke, not a dozen feet from where he had lain, into a dreadful pit of greenish darkness. He stood up to look into it, and found only misty emptiness. It seemed to have no farther walls, nor floor. He swayed back from it, giddily.

The scrape of a foot jarred his nerves. He spun apprehensively, and then grinned with a shaken relief when he found his two bodyguards behind him, safely back from the rim of that inexplicable pit, staring up at a vague blue flickering in the cloudy dark above.

'Aye!' boomed Hal Samdu. 'It's a ship.'

'And time we were rescued!' gasped Giles Habibula. 'Dear life knows we've been waiting long enough, dying in this wicked cold.'

'Giles!' Bob Star called anxiously. 'How did we get here? And what's this pit?'

'Ah, lad!' The fat man came waddling toward him, flinching visibly from the nearness of that dreadful precipice, yet beaming with a surprised relief. 'We thought you'd never wake, before you died of cold.'

The gigantic strength of Hal Samdu swept him to his feet. Clinging weakly to the two men, he felt Giles Habibula's sob of gladness.

'A long time we waited, lad. Mortal long –'

'The pit?' He peered at it blankly, as Giles Habibula dragged him apprehensively back from the brink. 'Where are we?'

'That's where the prison was.' The old soldier's voice was a thin rasp of dread. 'After the raiders had taken the prisoner away, a red light shone down from the sky, where their invisible craft must have been. Beneath it, the walls crumbled into nothing. The very ground turned into red fire, and sank away. Ah, lad, that fearful pit is all that's left of the prison and the garrison and the Legion cruisers that were lying inside the wall. I don't understand –'

'So he got away?'

Bob Star turned heavily back toward that strange chasm, feeling sick enough to throw himself into it. He had failed the Legion, and the consequences numbed his mind. Nothing mattered now. Dull, incurious, his eyes lifted to that fitful shifting glare of rocket jets burning through the clouds.

'It's landing near!' Giles Habibula was wheezing gratefully. 'The Cometeers escaped with the prisoner, and all the rest are dead, but we at least are saved.'

'Tell me,' Bob Star whispered urgently. 'How did we get away?'

'We didn't, lad,' Giles Habibula answered. 'The prisoner spared our lives – I don't quite know why. He told us he was really the great rebel, Orco – but I suppose you knew that.'

'I did,' Bob Star nodded bleakly. 'My duty here was to

kill him, if there was danger of his escape.' In spite of himself, he sobbed, 'But I – couldn't do it.'

'Hal and I were waiting for you in the corridor outside.' Generously, the old man nodded not to see his bitter tears. 'Of a sudden, my poor old nerves were shocked by a frightful alarm. Gongs were ringing, and men running half-naked to their stations.

'Most of them never got there. They fell, lad, struck down by things they never saw. And a greenish mist dimmed my own old eyes. My ailing body failed me. I went down helpless with the rest – perhaps a bit before the rest, for safety's precious sake.

'Yet for a time I clung to my dim old wits, when Hal and all the rest seemed to know nothing. I heard the clatter of locks, and saw those great doors turning. Then I could hear some sort of fearsome creatures passing through – things I couldn't see.

'Presently the prisoner Orco came walking out of his cell, speaking and making gestures to what seemed to be just empty air. He was answered by uncanny hoots and booms of sound, fit to freeze your blood. And your own body came after him, lad, floating – carried by something I felt grateful not to see.

'The prisoner pointed out Hal and me, and something came to lift us – what it was, I don't want to know. But we were carried from the prison and dumped here on this frosty ground – without a blanket or an extra jacket or even a blessed bite to eat.

'Near us was some great ship – there was nothing I could see, but I heard machinery running, and the clang of the air-locks opening. My poor old heart came near stopping when the prisoner spoke to me. His voice was right before me, but you couldn't see him anywhere.

' "You are Giles Habibula, the pick-lock?" he greeted me. "I bow to the fame of your accomplishments." He laughed a little, but in a way I didn't like. "I think we are brothers." '

'Then his voice went black with hate. "I believe that you two are the insufficient bodyguards of the cringing fool who calls himself Bob Star," he said. "I understand that he will be conscious again. Tell him that I have spared his life once more – to repay him for sparing mine!"

'He laughed, as if that were some sort of ugly joke. "Tell him you three are the only men alive on this continent," he went on. "Tell him it's five thousand miles to the sea, and nine thousand more across the ice packs to the Isle of Shylar. I'm afraid he won't live to reach it – but he'll live to wish he had touched that button."

'He didn't say what button, lad. But he laughed again – it was a fearful thing, that thick laughter from the empty air. And then he said, "Tell Bob Star I'm going now to repair a blunder I made – a blunder in the disposition of his mother."

'A valve clanged then. Something hooted and boomed – perhaps his new friends were calling him. The air-locks rang shut, and the green fog swirled, and the ship you couldn't see was gone – with not a jet to push it.

'For a few minutes there was silence. When I dared to lift my feeble head, I could see the marks the landing skids of that great ship had cut into the frozen ground. I had almost found the courage to get up and go back to the fort to look for help – it's a good thing I didn't!'

The old soldier shuddered.

'Because a beam of pale red light came down from the sky – I suppose from that ship. It cut through the clouds, and shone down upon the fort. A fearful thing to see! The walls dissolved into mist and sparks and fiery dust, and the very ground sank away, until the fearful pit you see was cut into the planet.'

Giles Habibula shivered.

'Ah, me, lad! The Cometeers are fearful enemies. I almost wish that rocket hadn't come back to save us. If we live to save Neptune, it will only be to watch mankind destroyed by weapons we don't know and enemies we'll never even see.'

'Don't say it, Giles!' Hal Samdu's gigantic fists were knotted stubbornly. 'If we live, it will be to fight for the System and the keeper of the peace. Come!' He turned impatiently. 'We must look for that Legion craft, before it goes away and leaves us.'

That unsteady glare of rocket jets had vanished in the clouds, but Bob Star had felt a faint shock when the ship struck the frozen plain.

'It came down too hard,' he whispered anxiously. 'I think the rockets were misfiring, from the way the jets flickered. I'm afraid it crashed.'

They stumbled through the bitter darkness along the lip of that chasm, towards where the jets had vanished. What they found at last was no bright Legion cruiser, but only a pile of twisted wreckage.

'Dear life!' gasped Giles Habibula. 'This is no more than the nose of some unfortunate vessel. It will never serve to carry anybody out of this fearful land. We're still to freeze and die here, as Orco and his strange friends planned –'

Bob Star was peering dully upward at the wreck. Great plates of armour were twisted and blackened, and massive beams projected through the torn flesh of the ship like broken bones. Ports were shattered, like eyes blinded. Rocket tubes were crushed, and a colossal proton gun had been hurled from its turret. This murdered craft must have been a Legion battleship –

His heart came up in his throat. He staggered back from the wreckage, and shook his head blankly. He saw Giles Habibula and Hal Samdu staring at him.

'The *Invincible* –'

Numbing despair had paralysed his voice, but he needed to say no more. The mighty *Invincible* had been reduced to this battered fragment. That meant that Jay Kalam's gesture of friendship had failed. It meant that the Cometeers had no friendly purpose – and now, since they had liberated Stephen Orco, that arch-traitor could defend them against AKKA.

'Ah, so!' Giles Habibula moaned bitterly. 'It's only a miserable bit of the great *Invincible*. And the coffin, no doubt, of poor Jay –'

'Perhaps he's still alive.' Bob Star clutched eagerly at that faint hope. 'His quarters were forward, in this section. And somebody must have been alive, to fire those rockets –'

'Before the crash,' the old man muttered. 'But now I see no sign of life.'

Yet it was he who spoke, after Bob Star and Hal Samdu had failed to get inside this fragment of the craft.

'Lad,' he asked, 'you say the forward valve is clear?'

'It is,' Bob Star said. 'But locked.'

'Then help me reach it.'

They lifted him into the wreckage, to the mechanism of a great entrance valve. He clung to a twisted beam before it, peering in the darkness at the lock.

'Ah, me!' he whispered sadly. 'Why must a fighting ship be secured like a precious safe? Have they no trust in the men of the Legion?'

Bob Star, watching, marvelled at the quick, deft certainty of the old man's pudgy fingers. He was hardly surprised when something clicked beyond the blackened armour plate, and whirring motors began opening the outer valve.

'Do you know, lad,' Giles Habibula wheezed triumphantly, 'there's not another man in all the System who could pick such a lock? The fact is that it might have troubled me – if Jay hadn't called on me to help his experts design it! But let's look for him.'

The bridge was dark and empty. They paused to read the last, neatly written entry in the log:

Wreck falling toward south pole of Neptune. Geodynes gone and rockets crippled. Will attempt to land at prison base. General order: The Cometeers are our enemies, and the Legion will fight to the end.

Kalam

'Jay!' Hal Samdu's great voice was booming apprehensively. 'Where are you, Jay?'

'In his den, of course!' Bob Star whispered suddenly. 'It's soundproof.'

He ran back through the chart room to the hidden door,

rang, and waited. The little door opened. Golden light spilled out, and then he saw the tall commander of the Legion.

'I thought I was alone –' Jay Kalam's low voice rang with a sudden joy. 'Bob! Hal – and Giles! I had given you up.'

He brought them into the luxurious simplicity of that long, hidden room, and closed the door. Hal Samdu's gigantic frame relaxed to the warmth of it, and Giles Habibula hurried back to the galley to bring hot food, but Bob Star could find neither comfort nor appetite.

'I tried –' he burst out suddenly. 'I really tried, commander!' He set down a cup of steaming soup, unable to swallow. 'But I – couldn't.' His thin face was twisted with a savage self-reproach. 'I'm just the coward Orco said –'

'Don't say that.' Jay Kalam shook his head. 'I'm too familiar with the effects of such devices as the Iron Confessor to blame you at all. But I wanted to give you a chance to test yourself – partly for your own sake.'

'Thank you, commander,' Bob Star whispered bitterly. 'But I failed! I let Stephen Orco get away, to plot the murder of my mother and lead the Cometeers against the System –'

'No.' Jay Kalam's voice was gravely decisive. 'If there is any fault, it is my own, for holding a standard of honour too high. Perhaps I should have ordered Orco killed. I know I should have let your mother destroy the cometary object.'

'Are you sure?'

The commander nodded grimly.

'The way the Cometeers received our attempted gesture of friendship proves that they are absolutely devoid of the high qualities I had hoped to find. But let me tell you!

'Not three hours after we had left Neptune, the telltale screens began to flash. There was nothing we could see with the tele-periscopes, but the gravity detectors betrayed an invisible object of fifty thousand tons, approaching behind us – as if it had followed us from Neptune.

'In hope of establishing peaceable communication, I

ordered the heligraph room to flash a signal: *We are friends.*
I am certain, from all the recent reports of invisible raiders,
that the Cometeers know us well enough so they can read
such messages.

'They are no longer our friends, however. Before we
had time to repeat the signal, the *Invincible* was caught by
some tremendous, unseen force. The geodynes were helpless
against it. Like a pebble on a string, we were drawn toward
that hostile craft.

'Can you conceive an invisible beam of energy, Bob –
a tubular field of force, a mathematician might call it –
strong enough to drag the *Invincible* against her fighting
geodynes, five thousand miles in five minutes? That's what
happened.

'Then a red light burned for a moment among the stars –
in the direction of that invisible ship. And the *Invincible*
was destroyed. All the afterpart of the ship was somehow –
annihilated!'

'Aye!' Giles Habibula put down his spoon long enough
to shudder. 'I've seen that fearful light. I watched it melt
the prison away, and leave that dreadful pit.'

'I wonder what it could be.' The commander rubbed
his lean jaw, thoughtfully. 'Matter can't be destroyed –
even your mother's weapon, Bob, must act in some way to
keep the universe in balance, even while it seems to cancel
planets out. I've been wondering what happened to the
ship and the prison. I believe I know.'

He nodded soberly, while the other bent nearer.

'Matter can't be destroyed,' he repeated softly. 'But it
can be transformed. I believe that red light was the visible
effect of something that dissolves atoms into neutrinos –
those tiniest particles of mass, that can pass through any
sort of matter undetected.'

'That must be the answer,' Bob Star agreed, a little
relieved to find any sort of explanation for that giddy pit, yet
chilled with colder awe of the unknown powers of the
Cometeers.

'Anyhow,' Jay Kalam resumed abruptly, 'some forty

men were left alive with me. I made no effort to stop their rush to the life rockets. The vortex gun was wrecked; we couldn't fight. I remained aboard alone.

'The six little rockets drove back toward the fort here – a tiny swarm of blue stars, dwindling swiftly in the dark of space.' His dark eyes closed for a moment, as if with pain. 'They had gone only a little way,' he said huskily, 'when that red light burned again. The little blue stars reddened and went out.'

Hal Samdu's big, gaunt face flamed with anger.

'So they murdered the survivors?' he muttered.

Jay Kalam nodded grimly.

'That is our measure of the Cometeers – and of Stephen Orco! For it seems from what you say that he is now their ally.'

Bob Star stood peering at him dazedly.

'Which way did they go, commander?'

'As far as I could follow them with the detector, Bob, they were returning toward the comet.'

'We must follow,' Bob Star whispered. 'Stephen Orco must be destroyed.'

'He must.' Jay Kalam grinned without mirth. 'He has certainly forfeited his immunity.' He shrugged wearily. 'I was hoping to get help at the fort –'

'But now there's no help for us,' Bob Star muttered bitterly. 'The only men on the whole frozen continent, without a ship –'

Hal Samdu broke in, 'Bob, we aren't the only men.'

'What!'

'Ah, so, there are others – enemies!' wheezed Giles Habibula. 'In this monstrous confusion of disasters we've had no time to tell you, lad. But some stranger came up to us through the fog, while you lay unconscious there by the pit.'

'Why do you call him an enemy?'

'He's no friend of mine!' The old soldier shivered. 'At first I thought him a chance survivor of the garrison, and I called out to him. The answer was a shot from a proton gun. The flash went wide, thanks be to the fog. Then Hal flung a rock, and the stranger fled, snarling and whimpering like a hurt beast.'

'Eh?' Jay Kalam seemed to catch his breath. 'You're sure this fellow didn't come from the fort?'

'Sure as death, Jay. I saw him in the flash of his gun, and I know it's many months since he was washed and shaved to pass inspection. A bearded, hairy, shaggy brute clad in faded rags.'

'Strange.' The commander whistled softly. 'I wonder—'

Chapter Eight

DEATH ON NEPTUNE

Bob Star asked, while they were still within the ivory-walled luxury of Jay Kalam's quarters on the wrecked *Invincible*: 'Can't we signal for help?'

The commander shook his head. 'The signal house was destroyed, with all the spare equipment in the stores.'

'But we can't just do nothing,' Bob Star whispered. 'If I had another chance –' He sank into bitter silence for a time, until a flicker of hope aroused him. 'Couldn't we build something that would fly, out of the wreckage?'

'I was satisfied to land it as safely as I did,' Jay Kalam said quietly. 'The best yards the Legion has could never put this mountain of broken metal back in space again.'

'Isn't there anything –' Bob Star had to bite his lip, to stop a sob of frustration.

'We must search, I think, for that stranger in the fog,' the commander said quietly. 'If he wasn't a member of the garrison, it seems likely enough that he might have some means of communication with the outside. Not a very hopeful plan, but I see none more promising.'

They had searched three days for that shaggy stranger, but it was something else that Bob Star found. He paused in the foggy night. The light tube wavered in his hand, as if the thin beam fled from what it had discovered. Giles Habibula crouched close to him, whispering apprehensively:

'In life's name, what is this?'

Jay Kalam and Hal Samdu came up through the freezing dark, and they all bent to peer at what Bob Star had found: bits of torn and bloodstained cloth, a little pile of frozen viscera, a few gnawed bones, a hollowed skull still covered with scalp and yellow hair.

'This green cloth –' Bob Star picked up a torn sleeve. 'It came from a Legion uniform.'

'Ah, so!' Giles Habibula's voice was a thin moan of terror. 'Some poor soldier of the Legion was eaten here by the fearful monsters of the dark, as we may be –'

'He must have strayed from the garrison – but I wonder what ate him.' Bob Star paused to peer around them in the greenish gloom, and he couldn't keep from shivering. 'I thought there was no wild life on this continent.'

Jay Kalam bent suddenly to pick up a bright, blood-splashed object. He turned it beneath the light. It was an enamelled lapel pin of white metal – the figure of a bird, grasping a tiny scroll. The commander leaned to study it, and his breath came out between pursed lips.

'No,' he said softly, 'this man didn't come from the garrison here. I used to know him.' He paused and straightened, gazing soberly out into the foggy dark. 'He had pale, timid blue eyes under that yellow hair, and his voice was soft as a woman's. He used to paint pictures – dainty little landscapes. He wrote what he thought was poetry, and read it aloud to his friends. It seems queer that such a man should die this way –'

'Who was he?' Bob Star whispered.

'Justin Malkar was his name – his men used to call him Miss Malkar. But only behind his back, because he was really a competent officer. His crew admired him enough to give him this pin, the last time his ship came back to Earth. A well selected gift. He was weak as a woman for such gaudy trinkets.'

The commander bent gravely to lay the pin back on a rock beside the scattered bones, and Bob Star said:

'I wonder what brought him here.'

'His weakness, I suppose,' Jay Kalam said. 'Stephen Orco's power. He must have been several years older than Orco, but they held the same rank when they were ordered to join the Jupiter Patrol. Orco soon dominated him. His ship was one of the first that went over to the mutineers.

75

Yet he wasn't a bad man; Orco simply understood and used his peculiar weaknesses.

'When the mutineers surrendered, Malkar's ship was missing. It was the *Halcyon Bird*, a powerful new cruiser. Orco told us that it had been destroyed by our atomic shot. We soon discovered, however, that Mark Lardo had fled upon it – Lardo was a wealthy Callistonian planter who had been Orco's chief lieutenant.

'We suspected that their plan was for Lardo to come back on the cruiser and set Orco free. For the last two years, the Legion has been scouring space for the missing ship, but this is the first trace –'

He looked down again, at the glint of that bright pin on the rock.

'But what could have attacked him?'

'I think we'll know the answer,' Jay Kalam said softly, 'when we find the bearded stranger who shot at Giles and Hal.'

He reached to unsnap the cartograph from his belt. He had brought that tiny instrument to map their movements. He opened the cover and peered at the record strip.

'We're nearly seven miles from where the prison used to be,' he said thoughtfully. 'Until we have more information, we must assume that Justin Malkar died somewhere near his ship. Our logical next step is to explore this vicinity, following a widening spiral –'

'Ah, so!' Giles Habibula nodded apprehensively. 'Let's get away from these bones, before that monster comes back to pick them!'

They tramped on again, shivering in the fog. Bob Star led the way around crumbling boulders, up frozen slopes, across shallow valleys of eternal night. Jay Kalam watched the glowing instrument, and softly called directions.

They had found no other clue, and they had swung back toward the shelter of the wreck, when Bob Star turned aside toward something looming in the darkness like another boulder. A vague shadow, it took on reality as he stumbled wearily toward it.

The gleam of metal checked him. He made out the black ovals of observation ports, and the bulge of a gun turret. A trembling hope took his breath. He heard Jay Kalam calling him, and ran back silently.

'Quiet!' he whispered. 'That's a ship—'

His words were cut off by a beam of blinding light that struck the frosty ground beside them.

'They heard us!' he gasped. 'Get down—'

They dropped flat, scrambling for cover behind a rock. A sudden sword of violet flame stabbed the rock, spattering incandescent fragments.

'Bob?' whispered Jay Kalam. 'Giles? Hal? All safe.'

'Aye, Jay,' rumbled Hal Samdu. 'But where are the others?'

'Bob?' the commander called again. 'Giles?'

But the frozen dark made no reply.

Bob Star, standing nearest the ship, barely escaped the flaming beam from the great proton gun. He felt the shock of it as he dropped, and saw the slender needle swinging after him, still faintly glowing from that first discharge, a pointing finger of death.

He scrambled desperately away from it, toward the ship itself. The needle reached the bottom of its travel, and flamed again. Frozen rocks exploded behind him, but the shock reached him only faintly. Safe beneath the reach of the needle, he ran back to the main entrance valve. An instant's inspection told him it was locked.

'Lad! Where are you, lad?' The frightened voice of Giles Habibula startled him. 'Ah, the wicked things that can happen to a poor old soldier of the Legion!'

Bob Star saw him scuttling toward the hull with a surprising agility, to escape the reach of that glowing gun.

'The first flash blinded me,' he whispered bitterly. 'I ran in the wrong direction, and now we're trapped against the ship. If we try to get away, they can cut us down.'

'Here, Giles!' Hope touched Bob Star again. 'Can you open this lock?'

77

'Perhaps – if you'll just be patient.' Giles Habibula fumbled in his pockets. 'Ah, here it is – the same bit of wire that let us into the *Invincible*.' He started toward the valve, and shrank back abruptly. 'But why, lad? Myself, I'm content enough to have it safely locked – and no fighting men rushing out to kill us.'

'Open it,' Bob Star said. 'If you can –'

'I can – if I must.' He was already busy with his scrap of thin wire. 'Strange are the wheels of genius!' he wheezed sadly. 'Never could I use my great gift in peace and comfort – when anybody sends for me to test a lock, within the safety of the law, it's apt to seem impregnable. My ability seems to sleep until the screen of danger rouses it. It is ever sluggard, without the tonics of haste and danger –'

Motors began to hum, lowering the outer valve.

'Well!' He retreated hastily. 'It's your own folly, lad!'

Bob Star sprang into the open chamber of the air-lock. Listening, he heard quick, cautious footsteps approaching along the deck inside. He flattened himself back against the curved metal wall, next to the inside valve, and waited breathlessly. The blunt nose of a proton pistol came into view.

Few such situations had been neglected in his very thorough course at the Legion academy. And he was master of all he had studied – until the situation where he must kill flung him back into the grasp of the Iron Confessor.

He caught that weapon and the hand that held it. His quick tug tumbled a thickset, bearded man out through the inner valve, into the narrow lock chamber. The stranger was twice his weight, but his long training told. His quick thrust found a vital nerve, and he tossed his bearded attacker out of the lock.

'Giles,' he called softly. 'A prisoner for you.'

Silence met him on the cluttered deck. He found the bridge deserted, the chart room vacant. He climbed warily into the darkness beneath the blazing searchlight, but the gun turret was also empty. The bearded man had been alone. He went back to the valves and shouted into the bitter night:

'Commander, the *Halcyon Bird* is ours!'

*

The prisoner was recovering consciousness in the icy mist, with Giles Habibula sitting on his head. 'I am the Viceroy of Callisto,' he was snarling thickly. 'I am Mark Lardo, friend of the great Orco. If it's food you want, I'll show you how to find it.'

Bob Star and Jay Kalam were in the bridge room, twelve hours later. Disorder and filth had vanished. The torn charts were patched and back in their racks. Bob Star was cleaning and inspecting the navigation instruments, while the commander frowned over the cruiser's tattered log. Hal Samdu, who had been clearing rubbish from decks and living quarters, entered to report: 'Jay, the prisoner in the brig is howling like a wolf.'

'I suppose he's insane,' Jay Kalam said. 'That wouldn't be surprising. Anyhow, we can't do much for him. Have you finished?'

'Aye, Jay, she begins to look like a proper Legion ship. Have you learned yet how she came to lie here?'

'Here's part of it.' The commander nodded at the soiled and crumpled pages of the log. 'It seems from these entries that Justin Malkar wanted to surrender, along with Stephen Orco. He expected no special immunity, but his conscience had overtaken him. He was ready to pay for his treason.

'He wasn't allowed to surrender. Mark Lardo, who had been Stephen Orco's court favourite, came aboard with a dozen of his armed henchmen. From that point, the entries are somewhat obscure. From the facts we know, however, it seems clear that Lardo was really planning to rescue Stephen Orco.'

He frowned again at the torn and bloodstained pages.

'The puzzling thing to me is how he knew the location

of the prison. It would appear from these dated entries that he knew it before the prison was built – as if Stephen Orco had been clever enough to guess where we would locate it!'

'Even that might be possible.' Bob Star couldn't help shivering. 'He always seemed inhumanly intelligent.'

'Anyhow,' Jay Kalam continued, 'it seems clear enough that Justin Malkar deliberately sabotaged the rescue attempt – perhaps to atone for his own crimes. The plan, apparently, was to land on Triton, which is almost uninhabited, and wait there until the chance came to rescue Orco – when he was moved into the new prison.

'That Malkar wrecked the plan seems clear enough, when you read between the lines. Though he was a competent officer, he managed to wander far off his course on the voyage out to Triton – deliberately wasting fuel.

'Until the end, he let the plotters believe that he was with them. He contrived to use up the last scrap of cathode plate and the last drop of rocket fuel, in landing here. Although the fort wasn't a dozen miles away, the estimated position of the disabled ship that he entered in the log is a thousand miles from here.'

His eyes lifted from the last mutilated page.

'The rest we must read from other clues. It seems likely that Malkar hoped to reach the fort and arrange for the capture of his companions. He failed – perhaps his sabotage was discovered. Anyhow, the vessel lay here without fuel and with very little food aboard – most of the supplies had been consumed during the wait on Triton.

'And Mark Lardo is now the sole survivor.'

'The remains we found –' Horror took Bob Star's voice.

'That carnivorous beast was Mark Lardo.' The commander nodded, his lips drawn thin. 'It would appear that he contrived to lock his companions outside, where the cold would kill and preserve them. His ruse must have been some story of a rescue vessel landing, but apparently he had no idea, until the Cometeers attacked the fort, that it stood almost beside him in this fog.'

'Ah, the cannibal!' Giles Habibula came shuffling feebly in, his face greenish. 'The galley's filled with human bones!'

Jay Kalam sat smiling sternly.

'The artist in the queer soul of Justin Malkar ought to be pleased,' he murmured, 'with the retribution he arranged for Mark Lardo. Listen to him!'

Faintly, from the distant brig, they could hear the ceaseless hoarse screaming of the madman: 'Don't turn me out! They are getting hungry – Malkar and the others. Don't turn me out.'

Shuddering, Giles Habibula closed the door.

'Ah, Jay, it was a heavy task you set me,' he muttered. 'But I've cleared up the power rooms, as you wanted, and inspected all the rockets and geodynes.'

All three swung toward him anxiously, as Jay Kalam asked, 'Are they in working order?'

'So far as I can see.' The old soldier nodded. 'But the cathode plates for the generators are all gone, to the last ounce. And the rocket fuel left in the tanks wouldn't move the ship a precious inch!'

Chapter Nine

THE FIELD OF THE COMET

Giles Habibula remained on guard, while the others tramped the frozen miles to the wrecked *Invincible*, and came back toiling to pull a makeshift sledge loaded with heavy drums of rocket fuel. Then the old man primed the injectors, and Bob Star, navigator, took his stand on the bridge. With jets roaring blue, the *Halycon Bird* broke free of the frost and soared through green dusk to the wreck.

For many hours, then, they laboured to carry cathode plates and more drums of fuel from the intact stores beneath the chart house of the dead *Invincible*. Giles Habibula scoured the galley and stocked it again, and before they were ready for flight he had a hot meal waiting.

'So now we're off for the Green Hall?' he wheezed gratefully, as they ate. 'To gather all the fleets of the Legion against this traitor and his monstrous friends –' He peered at the commander, and started apprehensively. 'We are bound for the precious Earth, or at least the Legion yards on Mars – aren't we, Jay?'

Sternly grave, Jay Kalam shook his head.

'I'd be afraid to try to go back,' he answered softly. 'In fact, I'm almost afraid to try to call any Legion installation. Because I'm afraid we *are* the Legion.'

'We –' Giles Habibula gasped. 'In life's sweet name what do you mean?'

'The Cometeers have destroyed the *Invincible* and liberated Stephen Orco,' Jay Kalam said. 'That means war to the hilt. They've nothing to gain by any more delay, and every reason for moving at once, with adequate forces, to wipe out the Legion and kill the keeper of the peace –'

'My mother –' Bob Star bit his trembling lip. 'What can we do?'

'I have been considering our action, and I have reached a decision.' The tall commander straightened, rubbing thoughtfully at his unshaven chin. 'We're going to take off at once, in the direction of the comet –'

'Please, Jay!' sobbed Giles Habibula. 'Don't make such ghastly jokes!'

'I think we're safer for the time being on a course toward the comet than we would be on Earth.' Jay Kalam sat looking at him sadly. 'With the keeper of the peace stalemated, our forces had nothing left to match whatever weapon it was that crumbled the fortress here into that pit.'

'Ah, don't say such things!' Giles Habibula squirmed and blinked at him. 'Can't we even ask for help?'

'Not without a grave risk that the enemy will intercept our messages – and answer them with that annihilating beam,' Jay Kalam said. 'It might be wiser not to attempt any signal at all, but I have decided that we must chance a call to the Legion relay station at the atmospheric engineering plants here on Neptune, as we take off.'

'And if –' Bob Star tried to swallow the croak in his throat. 'If they don't answer?'

'Then we must take the farther risk of sending a message to the Green Hall,' the commander said. 'I think the safest channel for that would be tight-beam ultrawave, through the Contra-Saturn relay station.'

'But the answer will take many hours –' Bob Star protested.

'No matter who answers – the Legion or the Cometeers – we won't be waiting,' Jay Kalam told him softly. 'If it does turn out that we are the only effective force the Legion has left, I want to keep in action. If we could only kill or recapture Orco, remember, that would still reverse the whole situation.'

Jay Kalam rose from the table, adding quietly, 'Please plot a course for the comet, at full power. Don't worry about hoarding any fuel for return.'

'But you tried it once!' Giles Habibula started to rise and sank back weakly, his pale eyes rolling. 'You had a ship with a thousand times our fighting power.' He shuddered apprehensively. 'Out there is the mortal wreckage of it.'

But elation was surging up in Bob Star. In spite of all the commander's forebodings, the means to escape bleak Neptune had lifted his spirits. He wanted the clean freedom of high space and the blood-hastening song of speeding geodynes – and one more chance.

'Shame, Giles!' Hal Samdu was rumbling. 'If we've any chance to destroy that human beast before he can harm Aladoree – let's be off!'

His angry glance fell dully to his fork, and Bob Star saw that his great fingers had absently crumpled the metal.

The commander sent him to the gun turret, Giles Habibula to the power room, and Bob Star back to the bridge. And they burst at last from freezing clouds into the clear immensity of open space. The power tubes were burning, and life came back to the cruiser's dead transmitter.

Using a narrow beam and limited power, with all the equipment carefully shielded, Bob Star called the relay station at the atmospheric plants. There was no answer. He increased the power and tried again, but all he heard was the dry hiss of static.

'That's enough.' Jay Kalam stopped him. 'We can't risk using more power, or wasting more time.' He gave Bob Star a brief message in code. 'This is my general order, reporting the destruction of the *Invincible* and the liberation of Orco, and commanding the Legion to fight to the last – if there is any Legion left to obey. Get it off to Contra-Saturn, and head for the comet at full acceleration.'

A dimly green, flattened ball, Neptune was falling away into a blackness pierced with stars and webbed with pale nebulae. Bob Star shut off the rockets, after that last message was sent, and cut in the geodynes. The sense of motion ceased, under that different sort of thrust, but the greenish planet dropped away with a magical swiftness, drawing toward the smaller ball of Triton.

Behind them, the far-off sun flamed bright but tiny in the frosty dark, shrunk to a splendid star. Great Jupiter and tawny Saturn were faint flecks beside it on the screens of the tele-periscopes. The smaller Earth could not be seen.

Bob Star was not looking back, however; his eyes were on the comet ahead. He was alone on the bridge. The only sound besides his breathing was the high-pitched humming of the hard-driven generators. The oval, pale-green blot of the comet absorbed his uneasy thoughts. What, really, was it?

What were the Cometeers?

Obviously, they were intelligent. Superintelligent. They were invisible, or could make themselves so. The armament of their unseen scouting vessel had destroyed the System's greatest fighting ship, and dissolved that prison-fortress on Neptune into nothingness.

Men knew no more of the Cometeers, but Bob Star tried apprehensively, now, to picture them. Could they be human? He wanted to believe they were, for their humanity meant to him the reality of the girl – or the vision – he had seen within the prison wall.

'Lad, lad!' old Giles Habibula had chided him. 'You're dreaming. I think your father kept you shut up in the Purple Hall too long, when you should have been out looking for such a girl to call your own, But you mustn't mistake your lovesick dreams for the truth.'

'Dreams!' he protested quickly. 'The girl I saw is as real as you are, Giles! And in terrible trouble – because, somehow, of Stephen Orco and the Cometeers. I still believe we'll find her, if we ever reach the comet.'

Jay Kalam, however, had been equally sceptical.

'If the girl you think you saw were real, Bob, she couldn't very well be a native of any planet in the System. We have no inkling of any scientific principle that would enable the projecting of such an image as you describe, without terminal equipment. You want to believe that she's an inhabitant of the comet – perhaps a member of some friendly faction there. But the odds against that are billions to nothing.'

Bob Star whispered, 'Why?'

'The forms possible to life are so infinitely various,' the commander answered deliberately, 'the structural adaptations of protoplasm to environmental influences are so amazingly complex, that on all the planets of all the suns of all the universe, there probably never was and never will be another race precisely like our own.'

Jay Kalam smiled at him, with a grave kindness.

'I'm afraid Giles is right, Bob. I think you should regard that incident as purely subjective – a product of your own unconscious fears and wishes, reacting to the stimulus of the agency that made you unconscious. Rather than human beings, the Cometeers are more likely something you wouldn't recognize as life at all.'

Bob Star stood watching the greenish blot on the comet in the tele-periscope, until the ship and the world ceased to exist. He and that great green eye were alone in space. And the eye was drawing him onward, into its own unknown chasm.

If the Cometeers weren't human, what were they? Tentacled monsters? Animate vegetables? Crystal life, prism-shaped? Or could the entire comet, he wondered, be a single sentient entity? Might its intelligence exist not in discrete individuals but somehow as an attribute of the whole?

Horror took root in his mind, feeding upon his own fantastic speculations. Trying to find escape from those terrors of his own imagination, he went back to the astronomical task he had begun at the Purple Hall: looking for that remote asteroid which had wandered from where it should have been. He failed to find it anywhere, but he discovered something else.

'Something's wrong with Pluto,' he told Jay Kalam, when the commander came to relieve him. A harsh rasp of wondering dread edged his weary voice. 'I've rechecked my observations a dozen times, and the answer is always the same. It is drifting out of its orbit – toward the comet! I know that sounds insane, and I hardly expect you to believe –'

'But I do.' The commander's dark face showed no scepticism, but only consternation. 'It fits in with the secret reports we have been receiving from the Contra-Saturn observatory. A number of small asteroids had been drawn from their orbits into the comet – perhaps by the same sort of force that grasped the *Invincible*. Now it seems they're taking planets.'

'If they can do that –' Bob Star stood voiceless, trembling with his fearful expectations.

The tall commander shrugged, with a grave acceptance of whatever might come.

'You're tired, Bob,' he said. 'Go back to your quarters and get some sleep.'

Bob Star reeled away like a run-down robot. He dropped, fully dressed, upon his berth. But sleep evaded him – because the green eye of the comet still watched him. It had followed him into his cabin, and it searched his very mind.

The thin whine of the generators was an eerie, hypnotic melody. His numbed brain broke it into weird minor bars. When it carried him at last into an uneasy half sleep, fear went with him. Nightmares came, in which the Cometeers pursued him, shapeless and unseen.

He woke again, with the distant screams of Mark Lardo in his ears, and stood his watch, and tried once more to sleep. For four such haunted days, the ship drove on toward the comet. At last, with a bleak satisfaction in his voice, he could report to Jay Kalam:

'In five hours, at our present rate of deceleration, we ought to reach the surface of the object.'

'If the Cometeers let us!'

Bob Star left the bridge. Too restless to sleep, he made a tour of the cruiser. In the power room, he found Giles Habibula sitting on the floor beside the geodynes, fat legs spread wide. Empty bottles lay scattered around him, and he was very drunk. At sight of Bob Star, he started apprehensively.

'Mortal me!' he gasped. 'You gave me a fearful fright, lad. My first fancy was to see some monstrous thing creeping in to destroy me. Ah, it's a fearful voyage!'

He fumbled among the bottles, and found one not quite empty.

'Sit down, lad, and share a drop of wine. The precious warmth of it will thaw a little of the cold terror from your heart. Ah, poor old Giles would have made a sorry soldier, Bob, but for the red courage that comes foaming from the bottle!

'It's a sad thing, lad, but the age of man has ended. Those monsters are to rule the System now. Perhaps we're lucky to be among the first to meet the Cometeers – to die before we know what they really are. But I want to meet them drunk.' He tipped up the bottle again.

Bob Star went back to the tele-periscopes, and watched the comet grow. The sharp-edged, greenish oval of it looked the size of an egg, and the size of a man's head. It spread across the black of space. It swallowed the stars; became a sea of green, overflowing all the heavens.

He and Jay Kalam examined it with every instrument the ship possessed.

'I can't make anything out of it.' The commander shook his head, baffled and visibly afraid. 'That green surface is a perfect geometric ellipsoid. It is absolutely featureless. At this distance, we ought to be able to see anything as small as a house or a ship or a tree. But there's nothing at all.'

'The raiders were invisible,' Bob Star remarked.

'And it may be that they live on the surface we see.' Jay Kalam rubbed thoughtfully at the dark angle of his jaw. 'But I don't think so. More likely, I think, that green surface will turn out to be a kind of armour – though of no material we know. The hull, let us say, of an enormous ship. It does move like a ship. Our next problem may be to get inside.'

And still the object spread. It had covered half the stars, when the alarm gongs rang. Apprehensively, Bob Star sprang to the instruments. He took swift readings from the glowing dials, and integrated the results upon a calculator.

'We've met a powerful repulsive field,' he told Jay Kalam. 'It's already absorbing more of our momentum than the geodynes are.'

He called the power room, to order the braking action of the generators stopped, but still that repulsion mounted. He called Giles Habibula again, to meet it with the thrust of the geodynes. At quarter speed – At half – At full thrust –

He turned at last to the commander, shaking his head in bewildered defeat. 'All our forward speed is gone,' he whispered hoarsely. 'We're drifting back from the comet now – against the full power of the geodynes.'

'That seems to show that the green surface is really a kind of armour,' Jay Kalam said slowly. 'A barrier of the same kind of energy, perhaps, that is drawing Pluto toward the comet.'

'Anyhow, we can't get through.' Bob Star straightened, trying not to show his sick despair. 'From the readings I got, that repulsion must increase to infinity at the green surface. Nothing could break through – ' A shrill scream of terror cut off his voice.

'It's the madman,' he whispered hoarsely. 'Mark Lardo.'

The bubbling shriek came again: 'They're here! And they're hungry! Don't – don't let them eat!'

Bob Star turned back to his instrument, to read the intensity of that repulsion again. The prisoner had been screaming at intervals, ever since his capture – though never with such an ungoverned abandon as this. He started, when he felt Jay Kalam's hand on his arm.

'Bob.' The commander's low voice was dry with dismay. 'I think there is – something – with us, aboard.'

He wanted to deny that, because it was too monstrous to be true. He had heard nothing, certainly. His eyes had seen nothing. Yet, somehow, even before Jay Kalam touched his arm, his mind had been shrinking away from some fearful, unseen presence.

'Look!' The cry burst harshly from his lips. 'The green – '

A greenish mist was obscuring the instruments before his eyes. His body tingled to a sudden, stiffening chill. All his sensations were somehow blanketed. Very faintly, he heard Jay Kalam's whisper: 'Is this what happened at Orco's prison?'

He couldn't answer. His body had become a clumsy, un-responding machine. He realized that he was falling. Dully, from a vast distance, he heard the thin mad screams of Mark Lardo:

'Don't let it eat –'

Chapter Ten

THE COMETEER

Bob Star picked himself up painfully from the deck of the narrow bridge. His limbs were numbed and tingling uncomfortably. A dull, persistent ringing faded slowly from his ears and left a dreadful silence in the ship. The screams of Mark Lardo had ceased. He realized abruptly, with a sense of sick defeat, that he couldn't hear the geodynes.

Jay Kalam was moaning, where he had fallen, and Bob Star bent to examine him. His body was queerly lax. The skin was flushed, and cold with sweat. Heart and breath were irregular and slow.

Bob Star turned back to the instruments. The geodesic indicators showed axial deflection zero, field potential zero. The ship was being flung away from the comet, helpless now in that field of repulsion.

'Our visitor?' Jay Kalam spoke faintly, from where he lay. 'Gone?'

'I think so.' Bob Star went stiffly to help him get up.

'What was it?'

'I don't know.' Bob Star tried to swallow the dry fear in his throat. 'I didn't see anything except that green haze –'

'I wonder if it really was a haze?' Jay Kalam was still swaying giddily, but a grave alertness had come back to his thin face. 'Or was it perhaps the effect of a radiation which short-circuits nerve fibres. Legion engineers have experimented with radiations that seem to do that.' He glanced at a chronometer. 'How long were we unconscious?'

'Perhaps ten minutes,' Bob Star said.

Jay Kalam sent him to see what had happened to the others. A stifled groan led him to the gun turret. Hal Samdu

91

was just dragging himself up behind the great proton needle, stiffly flexing his mighty arms.

'Aye, Bob,' he rumbled. 'What came upon us?'

'I don't know yet. Tell me, Hal, what did you see – or feel?'

Hal Samdu shook his head.

'I saw nothing. A monstrous shadow crept into the ship. Then the green mist was in my eyes, and I couldn't see anything. This stiffness seized my body, and I couldn't move. That's all I know.'

Bob Star was descending toward the power room, when a strangled whimpering led him back to the brig. He looked through the bars, at Mark Lardo. Shocked horrors spilled out his strength.

Gasping, trembling, he clung weakly to the bars, staring at the thing in the cell. Mark Lardo had been big – a shaggy, powerful human brute. But this shrunken creature looked hardly larger than a child. Its skin was uncannily white and hideously shrivelled. It lay inert on the deck, mewing feebly.

'Lardo.' Bob Star's voice was thick with horror. 'Mark Lardo – can you hear me?'

The thing moved a little. The shrunken head rolled back, and Bob Star staggered away from the bars. He had seen its eyes. They were sunk deep into that tiny skull, and queerly glazed. He thought they must be blind. Smoky, yellow shadows swirled through them. They were the eyes of nothing human.

Sick to the very heart, Bob Star stumbled away.

Even though insane, the Mark Lardo of an hour ago had been a man, massive and powerful, his great, wild voice ringing through the ship. This wasted horror was no longer human. It had less than half the bulk of Mark Lardo, and little indeed of the savage, animal life.

Bob Star stumbled down the steps into the power room, and stood swaying at the bottom. 'Giles,' he called hoarsely, 'have you any wine?'

Giles Habibula was leaning disconsolately against one of the geodyne generators. His fat arms were flung across it in a sort of sick caress. He was sobbing, and he didn't seem to hear.

'Giles,' Bob Star called again, 'I want a drink.'

He heard, then, and came slowly across the room.

'Ah, lad!' He was drunk no longer, but weeping bitterly. 'You find me at an evil hour, lad. My poor geodynes – like a dear friend murdered! I think we both need a drink.'

He found a full bottle, in a box that should have held tools. Bob Star gulped down half of it. He finished what was left, and wiped a forlorn yellow face with the back of his hand.

'I'm an old generator man,' he muttered huskily. 'But never did I run a set of geodynes so powerful as these were, and so sweetly tuned. They always answered my touch as if they were alive, lad. They sang me a song. They loved me, lad – more than any women ever did.

'But now they're dead, lad – dead. Killed and mutilated. Every coil has been cut into a thousand useless bits of wire. Every grid and filament has been twisted out of shape. The very cathode plates are warped, so that they can never be tuned again.'

'They look all right,' Bob Star protested.

'Ah, so,' the old man wheezed sadly. 'Their shining beauty is left. But the precious life is gone. I sat here, too full of wine – wine and caution – to stop the thing that killed them.' He turned to fumble for another bottle. 'But let's drink again, and speak no more of the fearful thing I saw.'

'You saw it?' Bob Star took the bottle, and pulled him toward a bench. 'Sit down, Giles, and tell me what you saw.'

'Let me drink, lad,' he begged hoarsely. 'Let me drown that monstrous recollection, for dear life's sake, while I'm still sane!'

Bob Star held the bottle from him.

'Ah, well, I'll tell you what I saw,' he muttered at last. 'If you think it may help us guard your precious mother. But it wasn't what I saw that froze my poor old bones. It was what I felt – the cold, foul breath of mortal evil.'

'Just what did you see?'

'The ache of coming harm has been gnawing at me ever since we left Neptune,' Giles Habibula wheezed. 'Even wine couldn't kill it, altogether. Suddenly, a little while ago, I knew that some fearful thing had crept into the ship. I heard Mark Lardo howling louder.

'I should have fled from it, but there was nowhere to go. And soon I couldn't move, for that green mist came and chilled my poor old body. I couldn't move a finger, not even to lift a precious drop of wine. Ah, so, lad! I was sitting here on the deck, with the bottle between my knees. I never needed a drink so much, in forty years of soldiering, but I couldn't get the blessed bottle to my lips.

'Then the thing came down into the powder room. I could hardly turn my dim old eyes to see it, for that paralysis. It came partly down the companionway and partly through the bulkheads. Even the metal shells of the geodynes were no barrier to it. It walked across toward them –'

'What was it like?' Bob Star broke in huskily. 'A man?'

'Don't ask how it looked!' the old man begged. 'Let's drink – and forget the wicked wonder of it.'

'Please!' Bob Star urged. 'For my mother's sake.'

'Ah, if we must.' His fear-glazed eyes rolled upward. 'Ten feet tall it stood. A thing of moving fire! The head of it was violet, bright and tiny as a star, and cold as ice, wrapped in a little cloud of purple mist.

'The foot of it was another star, hot and red, in the middle of a little moon of reddish mist. Between the violet star and the red one was a pillar of greenish light. Spindle-shaped. It kept whirling; it was never still.

'Around the thicker middle of the spindle was a broad green ring. Some crystal, maybe. It seemed solid – but still it wasn't too solid to pass through the bulkheads. That's the way it looked, as near as I can tell you. But the horror of it was the way it made you feel.'

'So that was how it looked?' Bob Star nodded bleakly. 'Now, tell me what it did.'

'It did enough to my precious geodynes, life knows,' the old soldier moaned. 'It was alive, lad. It was never still. The pillar of mist kept spinning. The two stars beat like hearts of light, in the little moons of coloured mist around them. Only the green ring shone with a steady glow.

'It came across the floor, lad, to my precious generators. The mist swirled out – an arm of it reaching through the solid metal of their cases. And the song of them changed to a fearful, hurt sound. It was their cry of death.

'The thing left them in a moment, and came toward me.' His fat bulk shook. 'I thought I was gone, lad. The creature was hungry – with a foul and noisome greed. It yearned for the life of me, lad. And it reached out with that green fire to kill me, the way it killed the geodynes.

'But then Mark Lardo screamed again.' Giles Habibula sighed. 'That's all that saved me, lad. The evil creature saw me to be an old man, weak with many infirmities, and my flesh poisoned with the wine. It heard the madman scream – I saw it stop and listen. And it left me, for the sweeter meat of a strong young man.

'It floated away through the metal of the ship, not bothering about the door. And I sat listening to that screaming. It changed, lad. The last scream was something to turn the blood to ice in your very heart, lad. And that was all I heard.'

Bob Star stood speechless, thinking of the whimpering, shrivelled thing it had left in Mark Lardo's cell. Giles Habibula took the bottle from his hand and turned it up. His yellow throat pulsed convulsively until the last drop was gone.

The creature in the cell was not yet dead when Bob Star forced himself shakily back. It was no longer able to move itself, however, because a dreadful disintegration had already set in. Seeing that it would not long possess any kind of life at all, Bob Star called Jay Kalam. They went voicelessly into the cell to gather it up, and nerved themselves to strip it of Mark Lardo's garments, which now were far too large.

By the time they had laid it on the bunk in the cell, the shrunken fingers and toes were beginning to come away. No attempt at medical aid was possible, yet the last sickening indications of life lasted for more than an hour. There was no sign of intelligence, but the expression of that doll-sized head and the whimpering sounds it uttered made Bob Star believe the thing was still aware of agony.

At last the smoky yellow went out of the eyes. They were left terribly white, obviously blind, and shimmering with the same iridescence that now covered the rest of the body. The thing moved no more. The glowing remains continued to crumble, until Bob Star and Jay Kalam rolled what was left into a blanket, and flung it out of the ship into space.

Jay Kalam spent two hours, afterwards, with a small specimen he had kept for analysis. He came back from his tests, with an expression of baffled unease.

'That wasn't human flesh,' he told Bob Star. 'Several of the elements found in the body were entirely lacking; others were present, but in the wrong proportions. The chemical structure of the protoplasm had been queerly changed.

'Something fed upon Mark Lardo,' he concluded huskily. 'It consumed some ninety pounds of his weight. The thing it left in the cell was neither human nor really alive.'

'Commander,' Bob Star whispered, 'what – what do you think it was?'

Jay Kalam frowned thoughtfully.

'We expected to find no familiar sort of life on that object. But I believe the thing Giles saw was, in its own way, alive. It showed intelligence and purpose. It moved. It – fed.'

His voice had caught, and his pale face stiffened, but he went on in a moment, almost calmly:

'It must have been, in a sense, material – it consumed ninety pounds of matter from the body of Mark Lardo. Yet it was sufficiently free of the ordinary limitations of matter to travel through solid metal.'

He shrugged uncomfortably.

'Perhaps we should have expected something of the sort,' he added. 'Because the Cometeers have obviously advanced far above us, scientifically – whatever their moral lag. They must be able to manipulate matter and energy, perhaps even space and time, in ways still beyond us.'

Bob Star stood silent for a time, clinging grimly to his old belief in the humanity of the people of the comet – for that meant, to him, the reality of the girl he had seemed to see in the wall of Stephen Orco's prison. But his faith in her existence died, before the silent horror that still stalked the ship.

'I've read an old legend,' he whispered suddenly, 'of creatures that were believed to suck the blood of the living – '

'The vampire.' Jay Kalam's dark head shook, as if with a helpless protest against what they had been. 'A feeble and inoffensive myth, beside the Cometeers.'

He paused to draw a long, rasping breath.

'We had wondered what they want,' he muttered huskily. 'Now I think we know. I think they have come to the System for – food.'

A harsh, inarticulate rumbling came from Hal Samdu. 'Fight?' he sobbed. 'We must fight, Giles, you must fix the generators.'

Tears shone in the old man's eyes.

'It can't be done,' he gasped. 'My proud beauties – they were murdered by the Cometeer!'

Bob Star returned with Jay Kalam to the bridge. 'We are now beyond the field of repulsion,' he reported, when he had taken observations. 'But we're still flying away from the comet at a high velocity, and helpless to do anything about it.' He laughed bitterly. 'With only the rockets – '

At that moment the telltales flamed red. The alarm gongs clanged. He spun to scan the screen of the bow teleperiscope, and gasped breathlessly, 'Asteroid ahead!'

Chapter Eleven

MURDERED ASTEROID

Bob Star's fingers swept to the rocket firing keys. The *Halcyon Bird* trembled to thundering exhausts. Blue torrents of flame flared into the dark void ahead, lighting the screens of the tele-periscope.

'An asteroid?' Jay Kalam whispered. 'You're certain?'

'I am,' Bob Star said, too busy to turn. 'The gravity detector shows a mass dead ahead. Millions of tons. The deflector fields wouldn't swing it an inch. But I've changed our course with the rockets – I think enough –'

'An asteroid – ' Jay Kalam paused thoughtfully. 'The condensation theories of cosmogony have indicated the existence of such tiny bodies at the fringes of the system. But I don't believe one has ever been discovered, so far from the sun. We're a billion miles outside of Pluto's orbit –'

At the tele-periscope, Bob Star had sharply caught his breath.

'I see it,' he cried. 'It's still far-off, and safely to the left –'

His breath caught, and he bent closer to the screen.

'What is it?' Jay Kalam whispered.

'The thing is only a tiny, irregular rock,' Bob Star answered uncertainly. 'Probably no more than half a mile in diameter. But I believe –' suppressed excitement crept into his voice – 'I believe it's inhabited!'

'Bob!' protested the commander. 'That's impossible almost. When it's so remote – uncharted –'

'The light-diffusion,' Bob Star insisted still watching the screens, 'indicates an atmosphere. And so small a body couldn't hold an atmosphere, without an artificial gravity-field, I'm sure –'

'Planetary engineering is expensive, Bob,' Jay Kalam reminded him. 'Especially when the equipment would have to be brought so far. It would have been nearly impossible for anyone to develop such a remote asteroid secretly –'

'There!' Bob Star whispered. 'I have it again, with a higher power.'

He looked around suddenly, his lean face shining with wonder.

'It is! It is inhabited, commander! I see vegetation – it has been landscaped! And there's a building – a long, white building! A ship lying beside it – a small geodesic cruiser. And an ultrawave tower on the little hill behind it!'

Jay Kalam's hand closed hard on his shoulder. 'Can you land there, Bob?'

'Land?' Bob Star turned from the screen to read the other instruments. 'I don't know,' he said slowly. 'Our relative velocity is very high. It would take a lot of rocket fuel, to stop without the geodynes.'

'We must – if we can, 'Jay Kalam urged him. 'For we're helpless, on this wreck. If we can land, we should be able to secure the use of the ship you saw. Or at least to signal some Legion base for aid.'

Intent over his instruments, Bob Star had seemed hardly to hear. At last he read the final integration from the calculator, and turned swiftly to the rocket fuel gauges.

Anxiously, Jay Kalam asked: 'What do you find?'

'I think we can do it.' Bob Star said. 'With just about enough fuel left to fry an egg. We won't be able to leave the asteroid again – unless we get the other ship, or at least a new supply of rocket fuel."

'Try it,' Jay Kalam said.

Again the rockets thundered response to the firing keys.

'I'll find Hal Samdu,' the commander said, 'and send him back into the proton gun turret. And you keep alert, Bob. Because I think we aren't very likely to meet a friendly reception. Honest folk are not apt to frequent a secret refuge a billion miles outside the System. Frankly, the asteroid puzzles me.

'The obvious guess is that it's a criminal hide-out. But it's pretty remote from any possible scene of operations. Pirates could hardly find it a convenient rendezvous. There wouldn't be much profit in running synthetic drugs so far. I don't know what to expect – except hostility.'

And even in that the commander was disappointed. Bob Star scanned that tiny world alertly, as the *Halcyon Bird* dropped upon it with rockets flaming blue; and Hal Samdu waited at his great proton needle. But no challenge came from the ultrawave tower. No hidden proton guns stabbed out. No stir of motion greeted the descending stranger. The tiny white spindle of the geodesic cruiser lay motionless upon the rocket field, beside the enigmatic quiet of the long white building.

The *Halcyon Bird* came at last to rest upon the level gravel of the little field, beside that other ship.

'Well!' Bob Star laughed uneasily, pointing at a fuel gauge that read *Empty*.

Jay Kalam was peering through the observation ports, with wonder on his face.

'Queer,' he whispered, 'that our arrival doesn't create some commotion. Strange ships don't land here every day.'

Bob Star looked out. Beyond the slim, bright hull of the motionless ship, he could see the white walls and pillars of the building. It was a vast, rambling structure, and every gleaming surface reflected expensive artistic simplicity. A tiny artificial lake burned like a flake of pale silver, beyond it, under the purple darkness of the star-pierced sky. And all about it slumbered the silent, exotic beauty of the landscaped grounds.

Such small planetoids are never round. The surface of this one was a maze of pinnacles and cliffs, ravines and chasms. Pale grass and rank, livid woodland covered the more level slopes. Many-hued lichens splashed the projecting rocks with green, scarlet and gold.

A slow smile of bemused admiration was creeping over Jay Kalam's thin face.

'Why, it's a fairyland,' he whispered softly. 'A dream!'

His shining eyes moved from one strange vista to another,

drinking in the peaceful, haunting beauty of lichen-painted rock-masses, the gay laughter of shimmering gardens, the cool smile of the silvery lake, and the simple welcome of the long white house.

Beside him, Bob Star felt a strange, painful joy stealing into his heart. Every shrub and tree called to him with a limpid voice of enchantment. The whole tiny planet reached out to him alluring, soothing arms of magic. They rocked his spirit in a cradle of peace. The rest of the System seemed abruptly very remote, the disasters of mankind queerly unreal. And he knew that it would be very hard to go away.

'Can't you feel it, Bob?' Jay Kalam was whispering again. 'Can't you feel the hand of a genius, in the balance and the rhythm and the pattern of every rock and plant and patch of grass. Can't you hear an artist singing, in the line and mass and colour of it?'

Bob Star nodded silently.

'This world is haunted, Bob, if anything ever was.' He went on softly. 'Haunted by the spirit of the man who made it. It calls to you from every vista – with joy or peace or laughter or pain. Or sometimes with terror, where the rocks are wild and dark, and those pale, livid trees are twisted like monstrous dwarfs.'

Something made him shiver.

'But it's dead. Its maker is dead.' His low voice carried a strange, half-absent conviction. 'He's dead, and his spirit is trying to call to us, from the beauty he created.'

Abruptly he shook his head.

'I somehow got that feeling,' he said briskly. 'But we've no time to be talking nonsense, Bob. We must be finding out what's wrong, here – why everything is so still. And seeing if we can get that ship.'

They left Hal Samdu watching in the gun turret. Cautiously alert, gripping proton pistols, the three others descended from the air-lock of the *Halcyon Bird*. The synthetic atmosphere of the tiny world was fresh and cold, sparkling with the fragrance of the gardens. An uncanny silence haunted it.

Quickly, they crossed the bare gravel of the rocket field,

toward the other ship. No name was painted on its tapering silver sides. It was small, but new in design, modern and swift – patterned after the latest geodesic cruisers of the Legion.

'A good ship,' Jay Kalam said. 'And her valves sealed, her ports closed, as if she were ready for flight.'

'Ah, so,' muttered Giles Habibula, in a feeble, apprehensive tone. His eyes were darting this way and that, with a furtive, nervous quickness. His seamed yellow face was pale, his fat limbs trembling. He contrived to walk so that he was between Bob Star and the commander.

'Ah, so,' he repeated. 'But it isn't.' He was pointing at a dark, oily patch upon the gravel, beside the ship. 'The drain valves to her fuel tanks have been opened,' he said. 'Her precious fuel has all run out to waste upon the gravel.'

'That's so,' said Jay Kalam, under his breath.

Giles Habibula shivered. 'I don't like this stillness, Jay. The place is too fearful silent. Ah, some dreadful hand has touched this little world, Jay. It's dead, Jay. Dead! And no longer any fit dwelling for the living!'

They had come to the sealed entrance valve.

'It's locked, Giles,' Jay Kalam said. 'Will you open it?'

'If you wish.' The old man nodded reluctantly. 'But it's nothing good we'll find within. The ache in my poor old bones tells me so. We'll find nothing but the ghastly tracks of horror.'

He fumbled in his big pockets for a scrap of wire, and waddled heavily to the lock.

Bob Star looked anxiously around him. Silence was sawing at his nerves. The long white house behind them was largely built, he saw, of native stone. But its white, inviting luxury had been expensively finished with metal, glass, and tropical woods imported from the distant System – its materials represented the peril and the enormous cost of many a voyage of billions of miles. Its dark windows stared at him vacantly. A depressing spirit of empty desolation came out of it, and touched his soul with a cold chill of dread.

'While we wait, Bob,' Jay Kalam said, 'will you take a

look at the ultrawave station? See if the transmitter is in working order. And if the automatic printers have been taking down any newscasts. It would take days to get an answer to any message, at this distance. But perhaps we can learn how the System has been faring.'

He hastened away across the tiny field, and up the cragged height where the spidery tower stood. Eerie stillness dogged him. It was hard to keep from looking behind him.

He pushed open a swinging door, and entered the tiny, rock-walled room beneath the tower. Horror thrust him back. Every piece of equipment in the room was useless. The receivers were dead. The printers were silent. The transmitter had been wrecked, as cleverly and completely as the geodynes of the *Halcyon Bird*. Every wire had been cut into many pieces. Every tube had been destroyed. The plates of every condenser were twisted, strangely corroded.

But the silent horror was shrieking at him from what lay on the floor. It had been a man. There were scattered garments. A little pile of grey, ash-like dust shimmered with pale, unpleasant colours. He saw dark stains, where some liquid had run. The Cometeers had been here before him.

He shut the door upon the thing within the room, and went shakily back down to the rocket field. Jay Kalam and Giles Habibula were still standing beneath the sealed entrance valve; he told the commander in a hushed voice what he had found, and asked Giles Habibula:

'You can't open it?'

'Ah, lad!' Sadly, the old man shook his head. 'Have you no faith in my precious genius? I could have opened it in a moment, lad – but I waited for you to come back. Old Giles is too old and feeble, lad, to be recklessly loosing upon himself such frightful evil as is locked within the ship –'

He touched the lock again, and humming motors lowered the valve. Side by side, Bob Star and Jay Kalam mounted it. On the deck within they found crumpled garments, piled with iridescent ash, and darkly stained where some strange fluid had run. Jay Kalam shrank back, shivering.

'Giles,' he whispered hoarsely, 'see if the geodynes are ruined.'

'But come with me,' the old man begged. 'Old Giles is no mortal fool, to go blundering off alone –'

Another heap of weirdly shining ash stopped them at the door of the power room. Giles Habibula peered with apprehensive eyes at the gleaming generators, and sorrowfully shook his head.

"Murdered!" he wheezed. "Destroyed, like our own. This ship is as useless as the *Halcyon Bird*.'

'The ship must have been about to depart, when it happened,' Jay Kalam murmured thoughtfully. 'The valves were closed, the crew at their places. I suppose the owners of the place were trying to escape. But they must have left clues for us –'

His slender hands had clenched, as if with sudden agony. A dark pain tightened his face.

'That's all that's left for us to do,' he added bitterly. 'To play detective! For we're marooned here, without any way to depart or to call for aid. There's nothing else we can do –'

Chapter Twelve

OUT OF THE WALL

For a time they stood in silence, upon the silent deck of the dead ship. Beside them lay the grey, glowing heap of something that once had been a man. A black despair had chained them to it, until Jay Kalam abruptly lifted his shoulders.

'The only thing I see,' he said, 'is to explore the asteroid, and learn as much as we can about the men who lived here. Perhaps we can uncover some resource. Perhaps there's a reserve of rocket fuel, or even a new set of geodynes. We can begin with a search of this ship. There may be documents –'

They found eleven more piles of glowing dust, where men had died. Two were on the small bridge. Bob Star left them, to examine the log. The positions entered in it told that the ship had made many voyages to Pluto, the equatorial colonies of Neptune, and certain of the smaller asteroids. But it contained no hint of the business or identity of her owners. Jay Kalam made a more perplexing discovery. He came from one of the cabins, carrying a ring and a little black book.

'I found these,' he said, 'in the dust where a man died. He may have been the owner of the ship; his suite was the choice one, and very elaborately furnished. I don't know what to make of it.'

He showed Bob Star what he had found. The ring was plain gold. It had a broad black set, deeply inscribed, in scarlet, with the outlines of crossed bones, and a looped tau cross. That same symbol was stamped in red upon the black cover of the book. Its thin pages, Bob Star saw, were filled with penned hieroglyphs, meaningless to him.

'It's a diary, I imagine,' Jay Kalam answered his inquiring

frown. 'The difference in the colour of the ink seems to show many brief entries, made at different times. It ought to be interesting, but it looks like some sort of shorthand, probably in cipher. I'll see what I can do with it.'

'Perhaps we'll find more papers in the mansion,' Bob Star suggested hopefully.

'I doubt it. The business of these people seems to have made them very cautious.' He was studying the ring again, and the red emblem on the hook, with a worried frown. 'This symbol is what puzzles me.'

Bob Star bent to peer at that curious design of looped cross and crossed bones.

'Was that the sign – ' His voice caught, and he began to tremble.

'That was it.' The commander nodded soberly. 'The symbol on that sealed magnelithium cylinder, in which Edwin Orco found the strange infant he named Stephen.' His pale lips drew stern. 'I think the secret of this asteroid will be useful to us – if we can only find it.'

They went on to the great, rambling white-walled house, and climbed to the broad veranda. Bob Star stepped shakily over the sinister glow of a pile of greyish ash, beside a wide dark stain and a discharged proton pistol. He hammered on a great door of wrought silver, which bore, in red enamel, the crossed bones of death and the looped cross of life.

Silence let them in, to meet the austere welcome of brooding death. Exploring the lofty, dimly lit halls, and the vast magnificence of deserted room, they were astounded again and again at the evidence of lavish luxury. One glimpse into the immense kitchen almost banished the apprehensions of Giles Habibula.

'Ah, lad!' His seamed face was shining. 'Here's abundance! Whoever he may have been, the master of this place knew the secret of life. No finer victuals and wines could be gathered from all the System!'

He gasped for breath, licking his fat blue lips.

'We need live no longer in that mortal coffin of a wreck,

Jay – save the one of us on guard. Life knows how long we may be marooned upon this gloomy rock. Forever, it seems likely. We may as well dine and drink – '

His voice died abruptly, when they came again upon the shining ash of another man.

In one vast, long, dim room, they found a great library of magnificently printed volumes. The lofty walls were hung with the work of famous painters. Niches were set with fine sculpture. An alcove held a fine optiphone and many thousands of records, which set Jay Kalam's dark eyes to glowing.

This was a secret kingdom,' he said softly. 'It was a great mind's dream of paradise, transmuted into reality by some extraordinary power of accomplishment. A shining light of genius is reflected everywhere: in the beauty that sings from the gardens, in the architecture of this building, in this wonderful room – '

'Ah, so, Jay,' put in Giles Habibula. 'And don't forget the kitchen and the precious cellar.'

'A true artist,' the commander went on, gently. 'A supreme creator – his mark is everywhere.' He was staring around with a baffled frown. 'And his capacities included a genius for anonymity: we haven't found a letter, a photograph, a memorandum – not even a monogram, except the one on the ring and the book.'

Jay Kalam had returned to the *Halcyon Bird*, to attempt to wrest the secret from the shorthand diary, when Giles Habibula made another discovery. Bob Star and Giles Habibula were crossing the library, when the old man abruptly halted.

'Lad,' he said, his voice thin and hollow in the vastness of the room, 'there's a hidden passage in the wall of the alcove, yonder.'

With a sceptical interest, Bob Star inquired: 'How do you know?'

'How do you know, lad, which way is up and which is down?' He sighed heavily. 'It's feeling, lad, a blessed instinct. A matter of subconscious observation. A precious

107

aptitude, refined by long training. Old Giles Habibula was not always in the Legion, lad. Before that night when a woman let him down, he was a free agent, living by his genius.

'Men can't hide their treasures from Giles Habibula, lad. For their minds work alike, as their locks do.' His thin voice sank confidentially. 'When you wish to find something a man has hidden, lad, merely consider the kind of man he is, the circumstances he was in, and you'll go straight to the hiding place.'

'Do you really think,' Bob Star inquired doubtfully, 'that there's a secret passage here?'

'Think?' echoed the old man, scornfully. 'I know it.' He pointed. 'That wall, you see, is thick enough to conceal a narrow passage.'

'But I don't!' Bob Star protested. 'It looks thin enough –'

'That's because the pillars and hangings are cunningly designed to hide the thickness of it – a clever optical illusion.' He was waddling towards the alcove. 'The entrance should be in that odd corner. It's well concealed from the rest of the room, and convenient to the steps within.'

His thick, deft, oddly sensitive fingers were rubbing and tapping at the richly polished panels of red Venusian hardwood.

'Ah, so,' he breathed. 'Here's the door. The dust, you observe, is broken in the crack.'

'I don't observe,' Bob Star said. 'But if you think it really is a door, I'll break it down.'

'Wait, lad!' Giles Habibula protested indignantly. 'It might be broken down. But there's no aesthetic satisfaction in the breaking down of doors. That's a crude admission that craftsmanship has failed. The very thought is a twisted blade in the heart of genius, lad.

'The means of opening the door are at hand, and we have but to lay our finger on them. A switch, no doubt, for the mechanism is doubtless electrical. The master of this house,' he said slowly, 'was elaborately methodical, and himself a great genius.' Heavy lids drooped briefly over his fishy eyes.

'Ah, so!' he wheezed. 'The optiphone, of course! Some trick with the dials – '

His thick fingers touched the knobs. Silently, the scarlet panel swung inward, and white lights flashed on beyond.

'Walk ahead, lad,' he asked. 'And keep your weapons handy. It's possible that someone is yet alive in the hidden space below. And life's too precious to be wasted, in any desperate encounter with proton pistols – '

Bob Star walked eagerly ahead, down a narrow, long flight of winding, rock-hewn stairs. He found no living thing below however. What he did find merely increased the haunting enigma of the asteroid. At the foot of the stair, cut into the very heart of the tiny world, was an enormous chamber. It contained an elaborate biological research laboratory. There were powerful microscopes, radiological and chemical apparatus, ovens, incubators and vats of ghastly specimens – most of them human. The Cometeers, apparently, had found the place as readily as had Giles Habibula. The dust of seven human beings lay shimmering on the floor.

Back aboard the *Halcyon Bird*, Jay Kalam listened to Bob Star's account of the find, with thin lips compressed. He didn't speak, and Bob Star asked: 'Have you deciphered the diary?'

'No,' the commander shook his head. 'It's more difficult than I had expected.'

Time went by upon the planetoid, each hour a new drop of bitterness in the cup of the four Legionnaires. One hope faded, and another. They found no signal apparatus, no spare geodynes, not even an extra drum of rocket fuel. The mystery of the lonely rock still evaded them. Jay Kalam reported no progress with his efforts to read the secret diary.

At last, from the bridge of the helpless *Halcyon Bird*, Bob Star watched Pluto approach the pallid ellipse of the cometary object. For many days it had been plunging outward from its former orbit. He waited with a troubled wonder to see it checked by that field of repulsion, but nothing stopped it. It struck that sea of shining green, and vanished.

He turned the tele-periscope back to Neptune. It re-assured him for a moment to find that next planet still in its place, but then he saw that the gap between Neptune and Triton looked too wide. The satellite was already on its way.

'Triton!' he muttered huskily. 'Then Neptune — and finally the Earth.' His lean hands clenched helplessly. 'But there's nothing we can do —'

That same night, he was striding restlessly, alone, through the silent gloom of a great hall in the white mansion. Pale lights burned cold on high walls panelled with black and scarlet. The white floor was hard white metal. He paused upon it suddenly, staring unbelievingly at a panel in the wall.

He had seen a moving shadow there. It brought back a shadow and vision that had come to him in the fort at Neptune, and a face that had not yet faded from his uneasy dreams. Trembling with eagerness, he stepped quickly toward the shadow. In spite of himself, he was whispering:

'Come back to me! Please come back —'

The shadows darkened and began to glow, somehow sinking back beyond the surface of the black-and-scarlet wall. A pure blue light was born among them, brighter than their flaming edges. His heart paused when they rushed together, and became a perfect, luminous reality.

It seemed to him as if a deep niche had suddenly been cut in the wall. Its shape was a tapered spiral. It was black. It flamed with innumerable lights, from scattered crystal flakes of blue. A many-angled pedestal of purest sapphire burned within it.

Upon the pedestal, as before, stood the girl.

Her beauty brought an ache to his throat. Her sweet body glowed white against the darkness and the sapphire flame of the spiral chamber. His first glimpse brought a confused and yet indelible impression of her straight, slim perfection, of the massed midnight of her red-glinting hair, of the pale, tragic oval of her face, and the wide, sad eyes of golden-flecked brown.

In a moment he saw that she was hurt. Her white robe was torn and stained with red. She swayed upon the vast sapphire. The pallor of pain was on her face, and her eyes were deep and dark with agony. He could see that she was fighting desperately against weakness and pain – and against something else. Bob Star sensed a terrific, invisible conflict, in which her mind was making some supreme exertion –

He started toward her, impulsively driven to her aid.

Two yards from the wall, he checked himself. She wasn't here. She was simply a shadow in the wall. She was no more here than she had been in the prison on Neptune, two billion miles away. Just a shadow –

Or not even that. Perhaps she was mere hallucination, the daughter of a brain that Stephen Orco had cracked with the Iron Confessor. The red hammer of pain, not still for nine years, still beat behind that scar – and it seemed to him now that the blue fire in the crystals behind the girl, danced in time to its beat.

He realized abruptly that she hadn't motioned him to keep away, as she had done before. Her tragic eyes were fixed on his face, anxious, pleading – and dilated with desperate effort. Reeling on the great sapphire, she held out her arms towards him. And her image flickered, oddly. It was just, he thought afterwards, as if he had been seeing her through a great sheet of some perfectly transparent crystal, and this barrier had been withdrawn.

He was startled then, to hear her voice. It was a low, breathless cry – but somehow relieved and glad. Some strange joy washed the pallor and the agony of effort from her face. Her slim body relaxed, and she fell toward him.

A shadow, falling? Fighting the numbness of incredulity, Bob Star sprang forward. He swayed with an utterly astonished delight when her warm, real weight came into his arms. For a moment she seemed lifeless. Then brief animation stirred her. She looked back toward the empty chamber, where sapphire flame still shimmered upward from the vacant pedestal. A curious call, a single liquid, bell-clear note, broke from her lips.

Immediately the sapphire exploded like a great bomb of light. Blue flame filled the niche. It faded to a swirling confusion of shadow. And the shadow died upon the black and scarlet wall. As if exhausted, the girl went limp in his arms again. He stood for a moment holding her, staring at the polished blankness of the wall.

'A shadow?' he whispered, and turned with her. He carried her back through the dim length of that great hall, and across the wide, columned gallery, and out upon the gravel of the rocket field, to the *Halcyon Bird*.

Giles Habibula met him, below the air-lock.

'Well?' he challenged the old man. 'Don't you think she's real?'

'Real enough.' The fishy eyes warmed with approval. 'And I'm glad to see you forgetting your sickly dreams. A good thing for you. Ah, and she's a lovely lass. Tell me, lad, isn't she fairer than your vision?'

'No.' Bob Star laughed. 'Because she is the vision.'

Staring, Giles Habibula gasped 'Where did she come from, lad?'

'Out of the wall,' Bob Star told him, and laughed again at his baffled doubt.

'Don't make fun of poor old Giles.' He straightened. 'Jay wants you,' he announced. 'On the bridge, right away.'

'Why?'

'I don't know, lad – but I can see that he's disturbed.'

'I'll come,' he said. 'But first I must find a place for her.'

There were vacant cabins aboard the *Halcyon Bird* and Giles Habibula waddled ahead to open a door and turn down the covers on a berth.

'What ails the precious lass?' he wheezed.

The girl had seemed unconscious. But the golden eyes fluttered open as Bob Star's arms drew away from her. Her oval face was strained again, anxious. She struggled to sit

112

up, clutching urgently at his arm. He tried to make her lie back.

'Don't worry,' he told her, smiling. 'Just take it easy. Everything will be all right –'

Her voice interrupted him. It was low, and husky with effort.

Bob Star shook his head. He could sense the liquid beauty of her language, but it was completely strange to him. He caught not one familiar word – nor had he expected to. Yet she turned to Giles Habibula, as if puzzled, disconcerted, by his lack of comprehension.

The old man cocked his yellow head to listen.

'Ah, lass,' he muttered, 'your voice is precious sweet. And it's evident you have something to say you think important. But your tongue is one old Giles never heard before.'

Still fighting a deadly weariness, the girl turned back to Bob Star. Her weary voice ran on, raggedly. Her white face was a mute appeal.

'I'm sorry.' He shook his head. 'But we can't understand. When you're rested, we'll find some way –'

Her fingers closed on his arm, with a convulsive, frantic strength. Her voice went louder, higher, and sobs were breaking in it. Tears of baffled frustration glittered in her golden eyes.

'What could she be trying to say?' Bob Star peered helplessly at Giles Habibula. 'When she came before, it was to warn me about the Cometeers –'

Her fingers relaxed from his arm. She slipped back to the berth again, unconscious.

'This cut on her shoulder?' Bob Star bent over her apprehensively. 'It can't be serious?'

'Ah, no, lad. Just a scratch. Rest and sleep will soon repair her strength. Old Giles will dress her little wound, lad. His old hands have yet a certain skill. Don't forget Jay wants you on the bridge.'

'Bob,' the tall commander greeted him, in a low voice which yet betrayed a suppressed anxiety, 'will you please

113

check the orbital motion of this asteroid, and our motion with respect to the cometary object.'

Jay Kalam stood watching, while he read the positions of the sun and Jupiter and Sirius on the calibrated screens of the tele-periscope, and bent to tap out his quick calculations.

'I see the answer on your face.' The commander nodded, at his expression of startled apprehension. 'It checks with my own. The asteroid has been caught in another tubular field of force. Apparently we are to be drawn out into the comet, along with the larger planets.'

Chapter Thirteen

FUEL FOR THE COMET

The cometary object hung close ahead.

To watch the last sunset, Kay Nymidee had scrambled with Bob Star's aid to the top of a high, bare pinnacle, beyond the rocket field. They were sitting, side by side, on a cushion of scarlet moss. Their feet dangled over a precipice.

Beneath lay the irregular convexity of the tiny world, moulded by the dead genius of its unknown master into vistas of fantastic, haunting beauty. Grassy slopes smiled with peace, and bright masses of flowering woodland laughed joyously. But above them, everywhere, rugged peaks and ridges stood solemnly and gorgeously strange in lichen-coats of green and gold and scarlet.

And the purple blackness of the sky was a vault of never-fathomed mystery. Day might illuminate the face of the asteroid, but never its sky. Now the sun was setting, behind Bob Star and the girl, a point of blue-white splendour, attended by the tiny flecks of Jupiter and Saturn. It cast black, knife-sharp shadows of the two upon the cragged opposite wall of the gorge.

Before them, above black shadows and flaming lichens, the comet was rising – for the last time. The ellipse of it came up like a featureless mask of hideous green, peering malevolently over the edge of the tiny world. Its leering face was near, now, and huge.

Bob Star caught the girl's hand; Kay Nymidee clung to him with an apprehensive grasp.

'*Temyo ist nokee*,' she murmured, in her own strange tongue. Her voice was deep and husky with dread.

'Yes,' he whispered, 'I suppose we'll soon be inside the

comet. But there's nothing we can do –' He checked himself, and forced a smile. 'But don't you worry, darling –'

Nearly a week had passed, since her inexplicable arrival on the asteroid; and now she seemed almost recovered from whatever ordeal she had undergone. The scratch on her shoulder was healed, her fair skin glowing again with health.

Through their efforts at communication, Bob Star had learned her name – Kay Nymidee. He had learned that her home had been indeed in the comet. He had found that she hated and feared the Cometeers – whom she called *aythrin*.

But that was all.

She had appeared disappointed and bewildered by the failure of the Legionnaires to understand her language. She had tried, desperately, to learn their own, making Bob Star point out objects, to teach her nouns, and act out the meaning of simple verbs. A brilliant and eager student, she could already make a good many simple, concrete statements. But anything more abstract than the greenness of grass or the sweetness of wine was still beyond her reach.

Bob Star glanced at her, and again her breath-taking beauty held his eyes. The sinking, distant sun, catching her head from behind, filled the mass of her dark hair with living gleams of red. Her face was a wide oval of white beauty, though now the green rays of the comet had overcast it with a look of strange foreboding.

Wide, golden, her eyes were on his face. In the failing light, the pupils were great pools of tragic darkness. They were haunted with consuming sorrow, with a sick despair that he yearned to brush away. But they lit, when he looked into them, with wistful golden light. A tender smile glowed for a moment on her face.

Bob Star caught her against him, impulsively.

'Kay –' he whispered. 'Darling –'

For a moment she relaxed against him, but then dread stiffened her. Her haunted eyes went back to the comet, and her face in its green light was once more stark and strange.

'*Mahnyanah –*' came her fear-roughened whisper. '*Mahn-yanah –*'

Bob Star released her.

'That's right,' he whispered bitterly. 'We can't relax for an instant, so long as Stephen Orco is alive –'

'Staven Or-rco!'

She seemed to clutch at the name, with a puzzling desperation. Her urgent voice repeated it, with that odd accent. Her slim arm swept out toward the fearful, rising face of the comet. And then she was talking furiously at Bob Star, once more, in her liquidly beautiful, incomprehensible tongue.

He shook his head, helplessly.

'Staven Or-rco!' He caught the name again, but that was all he understood. Her voice rose higher. Tears began to glitter in her eyes. She caught his shoulders, as if to shake him into understanding. But she gave up at last, sobbing in his arms.

The blue point of the sun had set, and the comet reigned. Its greenish, awful face spanned the dark sky from horizon to zenith. Visibly, terribly, it grew. Beneath its unearthly light, the great building was warped into an unreal palace of nightmare. Trees sprawled under it in black masses, like dark monsters crouching. The higher, barren rocks glittered beneath it like fantastic spires of ice.

The *Halcyon Bird* had become a green ghost-ship, when Bob Star and the girl came stumbling back to it. The others were waiting outside the air-lock, staring at the fearful sky. They looked ghastly; the strange radiance had turned their flesh lividly pale; their faces seemed like masks of horror.

There was to Bob Star something grotesque incongruous in the scholarly calm of Jay Kalam's voice, speaking quietly to Giles Habibula.

'Obviously,' he was saying, 'the Cometeers are able to generate and control some force analogous to gravitation. We have an inkling of the possibilities, from the geo-dyne and our own gravity cells, but their tubular fields of that unknown force have infinitely more range and power.'

Giles Habibula was nodding automatically, his face lifted toward the onrushing comet and ghastly in its dreadful light.

'They must have an engineering science a million years ahead of ours,' Jay Kalam's even voice went on. 'When you think of the tremendous power required to pluck a planet out of its orbit, or to drive the comet itself like a ship—'

His voice fell away into a chasm of breathless silence.

With appalling speed, now, the green edges of the comet were rushing outward. They were like green curtains dropping toward every horizon. Bob Star had to swallow, to find his voice. It sounded harsh and rasping in the dreadful silence. He asked Jay Kalam:

'Shall we go aboard?'

'If you wish,' the commander answered quietly. 'The ship is helpless; I don't know that it offers any sort of safety. I don't know what the danger is. You may do what you wish. For myself I'm going to stay out here on the field, so that I can watch until – whatever happens.'

Bob Star caught Kay Nymidee's arm, and drew her a little toward the air-lock. But she shook her head, and looked up again at the expanding sea of the comet. Waiting beside her Bob Star had a sudden unpleasant sensation that the asteroid was falling, with their bodies beneath – falling into a tremendous green abyss. The pale, sharp edges of it rushed down to the horizon, and the whole sky was a dome of flaming green.

He heard Jay Kalam whisper: 'We're about to strike that green barrier.'

A thin wail quavered from the lips of Giles Habibula.

'A frightful time!' he sobbed. 'What use is genius now?'

Bob Star put his arms around Kay Nymidee, and moved her a little into the shelter of the shining ship. What would happen when they struck? Would they ever know?

He waited, breathless. He could feel the quick beat of

the girl's heart, against his side. There was an odd little
flicker in the green vault of the sky. But nothing happened.
Waiting became unendurable. Shakily, he whispered:

'When, Jay? When –'

He heard Jay Kalam draw a deep, even breath.

'We've passed the green barrier,' the commander said.
'We're already inside the comet. Just look at the sky!'

Bob Star walked unsteadily beside Kay Nymidee, away
from the hull of the *Halcyon Bird*. His bewildered eyes
swept the sky. It still was green, an inverted bowl of pale,
weird-hued flame. But it was swarming, now, with strange
heavenly bodies.

His startled glance swept them. They were mottled discs
like dark moons, strung across the green. They were of
many sizes, coloured with a thousand merging shades of red,
orange, yellow, and brown, all splashed with an eerie
green. They were clustered planets, crowding the green sky.
The patches were continental outlines. The vast areas of
green, he thought, must be seas, reflecting the sky.

'A sun!' Jay Kalam was gasping. 'A captive sun!'

And following his gravely pointing arm, Bob Star saw a
great ball of purple flame. Its hot colour was fantastically
strange, against the green. It was huge – it looked three
times the size of the System's sun, as seen from his home
on Phobos.

Kay Nymidee had stepped quickly a little away from
him. Her slender white arm, trembling, was pointing at one
of the swarming dark planets, which was not mottled like
the rest, but a smooth disc of indigo. Between that planet
and the captive sun, Bob Star saw three glowing, purple
lines.

'Bob, Jay! Hal, Giles!' The girl was calling them all by
their names, softly accented. And still she was pointing at
that featureless disc of violet-blue. '*Aythrin!*' she cried
urgently. 'Staven Or-rco!'

She ran to touch the green-glinting hull of the *Halcyon
Bird*, and then gestured as if it had risen toward the indigo
world.

'Staven Or-rco,' she repeated, and ground her small hands together, as if obliterating something.

'See!' Bob Star whispered. 'She wants us to go to that blue planet. Stephen Orco is there, with the Cometeers – she calls them *aythrin*. She wants us to go there, and kill him.'

The girl had watched him as he spoke, brown eyes shining. Now she seized his arm, speaking at him furiously in her own language. She nodded, shook her head, shrugged, made faces, gesticulated. Bob Star put his hands on her shoulders, to try to calm her.

'It's no use,' he told her. 'We can't understand. And we can't fly the *Halcyon Bird*, if that's what you want –'

'She has something more to tell us,' said the commander. 'I wonder if she couldn't draw it?'

He found writing materials in his pockets, and thrust them into her hands. Eagerly, she drew a circle, and pointed at the great indigo disc. Then she made some marking within the circle, and held out the paper, talking rapidly again.

'The circle means the planet,' Bob Star said. 'But the marking inside –'

He had to shake his head, as the others did. And tears of frustration came suddenly into her eyes. She flung the paper down, with an angry, bewildered gesture, and burst into stormy tears.

'It's too bad,' Jay Kalam shook his dark head, regretfully. 'I'm willing to grant, now, Bob, that she's a native of the comet – although her humanity seems contrary to orthodox science. It's likely enough that she came to bring us information of some sort about the Cometeers and Stephen Orco.

'But nothing she knows is going to help us. Without any common background of languages or culture, or even of thought-forms, it would take her months or years, brilliant as she evidently is, to learn enough English to convey any complex or abstract ideas.'

He turned abruptly, and squinted at the purple sun.

'We must go aboard, Bob,' he said, 'and take what observations we can. We must discover as much as we can about the comet – and what is happening to us.' Something mushed his voice. 'I think,' he added, 'that we won't have much time for observations.'

'Why?'

'I believe the asteroid is falling into that captive sun.'

For a time, on the bridge, they worked silently. Bob Star was speechless with the ever-renewed impact of the comet's wonder. It was Jay Kalam, still gravely collected, who began to put their discoveries into words.

'This object we've called a comet,' he began quietly, 'is a swarm of planets. We've counted one hundred and forty-three. Since we entered on the forward side of the asteroid, we must have seen them nearly all. We knew already, from its gravitational effect on the System, that the comet's mass is nearly a thousand times that of Earth. The captive sun accounts for rather less than half of it. The average mass of the planets, then, must be over three times that of Earth. They've been built into a ship. The green barrier is the hull – an armour of repulsive force. The planets are arranged inside of it, spaced about a great ellipsoid –'

'What I don't see is how such a system could be stable.' Bob Star looked up uncomfortably. 'Such great masses, so closely crowded – what keeps them from collision?'

'They must be held in place with those same tubular fields – beams of force, set to balance gravity. The frame, so to speak, of the ship.' The commander spoke deliberately, half absently, as if to set his own ideas in order. 'The captive sun is at one focus of the ellipsoid. The planet which disturbs Kay so much is at the other –'

'And look at it!' Bob Star was peering at the screen of a tele-periscope. 'The surface of it seems absolutely smooth, but look at those machines! A little bit like our proton needles – but they must be enormous, to be visible at this distance! One of them stands under each one of those three purple beams, between the planet and the captive sun –'

'I believe I get it!' Jay Kalam's low voice quivered with

121

restrained excitement. 'That captive sun can't be any ordinary star – not with that purple colour. I believe it's artificial – an atomic power plant.

'That triple beam is probably the transmission system that taps its power. And, if that's true, the blue planet must be the control room of the ship. Those smaller machines around the three large ones probably distribute the energy to operate it.

'It must take enormous power, to hold and propel all these planets and protect them with that barrier of repulsion. Atomic fission wouldn't be enough. That plant must annihilate matter –'

His breath caught and his lean face tightened.

'I couldn't find Pluto, among all those planets,' he whispered hoarsely. 'I think that's the reason why.'

Bob Star peered at him blankly.

'I think the Cometeers wanted it for fuel,' he said. 'I think they have already stripped it of whatever they wanted to preserve, and flung what was left into that atomic furnace.'

He was silent for a little time. His face looked haggard and rigid as a mask of death.

'That seems to complete our picture of the Cometeers.' His voice remained oddly calm. 'They are universal marauders. They rove space from sun to sun. They pillage planets, and feed upon the life they find. They seize the planets themselves, to build into the swarm, or to burn for fuel –'

'And that's what they want with this asteroid?' Bob Star shivered.

'I think so.' Jay Kalam nodded, curiously quiet. 'The Cometeers have already once raided the asteroid. Probably they have no further interest in it, except as a speck of fuel.' Absently, he was stroking his lean jaw. He asked presently, very softly, 'How long have we, Bob?'

Bob Star remained standing for a moment in a dark reverie; he started nervously, and turned to busy himself hastily with tele-periscope, calculator, and chronometer. He straightened at last, and wiped cold sweat from his forehead.

'Three hours –' he whispered, huskily. 'Just three hours –'

Chapter Fourteen

ORCO'S VOICE

Jay Kalam closed the door of the bridge room with a weary finality. For a moment he leaned heavily against it. Then, with dragging feet, he followed Bob Star across the deck and out through the open airlock.

Kay Nymidee and Hal Samdu and Giles Habibula were still outside, on the gravel of the rocket field, beside that deserted mansion. They looked ghost-like in the pale green radiance that shone from all the sky.

Hal Samdu stood bolt upright. His great, gnarled hands were clenching and opening again, convulsively. His shaggy head was flung back, and his blue eyes were fixed upon the indigo disc of the master planet. His rugged face was grimly savage.

'If Stephen Orco is there,' he was rumbling, harshly, 'we must go after him – and kill him. For Aladoree –'

Giles Habibula and Kay Nymidee sat side by side on the gravel. The girl was marking little diagrams with her finger, on the ground, and talking urgently at the old man. He was patiently listening, wearily shaking his head.

'Old Giles is sorry, lass,' he said gently. 'But it's no use –'

They all looked up, when Jay Kalam and Bob Star came down from the valve.

'Well, Jay?' boomed Hal Samdu. 'Now we are within the comet, with Stephen Orco. How shall we move to kill him?'

Jay Kalam stepped back a little, wearily, to lean against the green-washed hull of the *Halcyon Bird*. His dark eyes closed for a moment, and his long face, in that unearthly light, became a stiff mask of pain.

'Still, Hal,' he said slowly, 'there's nothing we can do.'

He looked at Giles Habibula and the girl with weary pity.

'In three hours,' he said, 'the asteroid will fall into that atomic furnace. We still have no means to leave it.'

Hal Samdu's massive face twitched to a spasm of pain. Brokenly, he gasped. 'Aladoree –'

Giles Habibula surged apprehensively to his feet. His bald head rolled back, his small eyes peering fearfully at that growing ball of purple fire.

'Just three hours?' he gasped convulsively. 'For life's sake, Jay, can't you give us more than that?' His eyes rested for a moment on the commander's stiff face, and he shook his head. 'Poor old Giles!' he sobbed. 'What a reward for all his genius, and his life of faithful service to the Legion and the System – to be burned for fuel, within the bowels of a monstrous comet!'

He blinked his eyes and blew his nose.

'Wine,' he whispered. 'There's wine in the house. Precious, potent, ancient wine – chosen and aged by that other genius who used to own this rock. Fine old wine, too rare to burn for fuel –'

A vague smile smoothed the apprehension from his face, and he lumbered heavily away toward the great white mansion. Listening, Bob Star caught the faintly whistled notes of a sad but lively ballad of the Legion, *The Sparrow of the Moon*.

Hal Samdu was still standing rigid, watching the indigo planet. The muscles of his angular, weather-beaten face were working; he was muttering inaudibly. The commander's tall body sagged against the hull of the *Halcyon Bird*, as if the life had gone out of it. Bob Star swung to Kay Nymidee, who was looking from him to the purple sun, with apprehensive bewilderment.

'Come on, Kay,' he said huskily. 'Let's walk.'

She smiled. '*Se*,' she said softly. '*Ahndah*.'

They crossed the level of the rocket field, and climbed up into a welter of rocks beyond. The incrusting lichens had changed colour strangely under that green sky, so that the wild peaks were fantastic as the spires of a fairy city.

Bob Star made her sit beside him on a mossy ledge. His arms closed around her. He could feel her trembling. Staring away into the green sky, her eyes great pools of sombre dread. They were lost, bewildered, helplessly riding a dead world to doom. Yet he drew her close to him, and tried to think only of her white beauty –

Giles Habibula was beneath them among the rocks, panting with excitement.

'Come, lad!' he puffed. 'The dalliance of love is the food and drink of youth, I know. But it must await a time less torn with mortal urgency. Come!'

'What's wrong now?' Bob Star made no move to rise, for nothing mattered, now.

'Jay bids you come and aid us to load the *Halcyon Bird* with rocket fuel.'

'Rocket fuel!' exclaimed Bob Star, dazedly. 'There's none.'

'But there is!'

Bob Star helped the girl down from the ledge, and they followed Giles Habibula.

'Where –' he whispered breathlessly. 'Where did Jay find rocket fuel?'

'Ah, lad!' The old man shook the bald dome of his head, which shone greenish in the light of the comet. 'Ever the same is the fate of genius: it stumbles unknown into an unmarked grave. It wasn't Jay who found the precious fuel. It was poor old Giles Habibula.'

'How did you find it?'

'Poor old Giles had started to seek wine with which to pull the fearful fangs of death. But, beneath this mortal green sky, his aged spirit, weak and feeble as it is, rebelled against extinction. Ah, so! His precious genius awoke to the shocking touch of peril, and refused to be destroyed. It recalled Jay's theory that the owners of the asteroid must have hidden their fuel away against space pirates. It recalled the nature of that other genius who built this place.'

'Ah, and it set his old finger on the hidden fuel!'

They were crossing the rocket field. The old man's fat arm pointed toward the switch-box, built in the wall of the white house, which controlled the flood-lights.

'I simply walked to that box, lad, and opened it. There is a deftness that lingers in my old hands, lad. I found the secret of the box, that would have evaded any other. And there's the fuel!'

They came around the green-bathed hull of the *Halcyon Bird*. Beyond, not a dozen yards from her air-lock, a little cylindrical metal house had risen through the gravel. Hal Samdu was rolling black drums of rocket fuel from the door of it.

Bob Star ran to aid him. No more than two hours later, Bob Star, with the commander and Kay Nymidee, climbed to the bridge of the *Halcyon Bird*. Urgently, the girl pointed through an observation port, at the indigo disc of the master planet.

'*Aythrin!*' her soft voice cried eagerly. 'Staven Or-rco! We go?'

The commander turned to Bob Star. 'Can we make it?'

'We can try.'

His fingers touched the firing keys. Blue jets washed the gravel field, and roared against the white columns of the deserted mansion. The *Halcyon Bird* was alive again, and away into the green chasm of the comet. The asteroid fell behind them, to dwindle and vanish against the ominous face of the purple sun.

Bob Star felt a pang of regret, at its destruction. For it was in the cradle of its haunting, exotic beauty that he had come to know Kay Nymidee. His love for her had spread, somehow, to its laughing groves and the wild splendour of its lichen-painted rocks and the peace of the long white house above the smiling lake.

He thought unhappily that now its mystery could never be solved. After days of effort, Jay Kalam had confessed that he had failed to decipher the book that seemed to be a diary. The anonymity of its unknown writer was now forever secure. The purpose of that hidden laboratory, the meaning of the looped cross of life above the crossed bones of death, the possible connection between the asteroid and Stephen Orco – those riddles were beyond answer now.

'Have we fuel enough,' the commander was asking, 'to reach the master planet?'

'The tanks aren't half full, but we had time to load no more.' Bob Star was silent for a time, frowning as he read the calibrated screens and tapped out his calculations. 'I believe we can do it –'

His voice caught, as the telltales flashed and the gongs began to ring. Startled, he swung back to the instruments.

'The power beam – if that's what it is,' he whispered huskily. 'Between the planet and that atomic engine. It has caught us, with its own field of force. A danger I hadn't expected.'

He paused to read the screens again, and swiftly calculated a new course for the ship.

'I think we can keep free, but this costs fuel.' Checking his figures again, he shook his head and bit his lip. 'I'm afraid we'll land a little too hard for comfort.'

Stern-faced, abstracted, he turned again to screens and calculator, fighting a silent battle to conserve every precious drop of fuel.

In hours, perhaps the flight was long. But always it seemed to Bob Star that they had hardly left the asteroid, before the *Halcyon Bird* was slanting down out of a pallidly green sky that swarmed with many-coloured worlds, toward the dark, strangely level surface of the master planet.

That great world seemed a perfect sphere of indigo, unbroken by mountain or sea. It appeared absolutely featureless, save for the overwhelmingly colossal machines, red and mysterious beneath their pale domes of greenish radiance, that scattered it at distances of hundreds or thousands of miles.

As that dark, strangely forbidding surface expanded

before them, Kay Nymidee pointed through an observation port at the looming bulk of one of those machines.

'Go –' she said eagerly, and groped for a word, 'there!'

Bob Star nodded, and set the nose of the *Halcyon Bird* toward it. Then he looked doubtfully at a fuel gauge.

'I'll try,' he whispered.

But the needles crept inexorably towards zero. The even drumming of the rockets was interrupted by a warning cough. He shook his head, and brought the *Halcyon Bird* to a jarring landing upon the strange flatness of the indigo world, with rockets dead before the ship was still.

'The tanks are empty,' he muttered blankly. 'The ship won't move again.'

Kay Nymidee seized his shoulder, and pointed imploringly at the crimson, cyclopean mass of the machine ahead, a bewildering and fantastic enigma of red metal, within its transparent shell of shimmering green.

'Sorry, Kay.' He shook his head again. 'We just couldn't make it.'

The mute reproach in her brown eyes changed slowly to frightened dismay.

'Perhaps we can walk, if we aren't discovered,' Jay Kalam suggested hopefully. 'Kay seems determined to take us to the machine. And it doesn't look so far –'

'The distance is deceptive,' Bob Star told him, 'because of the vast size of the planet, and the remarkable clearness of the atmosphere, and the lack of any other object for comparison.'

'How far is it?'

Bob Star looked at his instruments.

'According to my last observation,' he said, at last, 'that machine is about a hundred and twenty miles from us.'

The hostile impact of an alien world struck the five with shocking violence, when they left the air-lock of the useless *Halcyon Bird*. It was five hours later. They had spent the time in preparing to undertake a desperate march of more than a hundred miles. Bob Star and Hal Samdu were dragging two sledges improvised from metal doors torn from within the ship, packed with food, water, and weapons.

The runners sang musically across the flat infinity of the planet's surface. The puzzling substance of it was absolutely smooth, hard and slippery underfoot. Nowhere, so far as they could see, was it broken by any irregularity. At first they found walking difficult; Giles Habibula fell sprawling twice. As a compensatory advantage, however, the sledges, once started, glided along with little effort.

'A whole world, armoured?' marvelled Bob Star. 'Is it metal?'

'It isn't metal.' Jay Kalam shook his head. 'I took time to examine it, after I finished those atmospheric tests – though I still don't know what it is.' He shrugged uneasily. 'Something harder than diamond and tougher than steel. Acids don't affect it. It neither absorbs nor radiates heat. Perhaps it isn't actually matter at all, but another stable energy-field, more or less like that green barrier.'

Surprisingly, his tests had found a breathable atmosphere. A rich oxygen content made up for the low barometric pressure. The surface gravitation, Bob Star had reported, was slightly less than Earth-standard. Since the planet had four times the diameter of Earth, that meant that its relative density must be extremely low.

At a little distance from the *Halcyon Bird*, Jay Kalam paused, and they all looked back. The silvery cruiser lay small and lonely upon that blue, jewel-smooth plain. It was the only object upon the infinite world behind, a solitary gleam under the pale green sky.

Blue flame, as they looked, gushed suddenly from the gun turret. The bright hull glowed swiftly red, and flames exploded from the ports. The five went on, regretful, for it had been a faithful ship.

'They'll surely find the wreck,' Jay Kalam said. 'but I hope they'll think we died in it.'

They plodded on, wearily dragging the sledges, toward

the red riddle of that enormous machine, a hundred miles away. Bob Star's eyes rested on it, with an apathetic fascination. It stood on a square platform, which might be, he estimated two miles high and ten in length. The machine towered above it, so immense that he dared not attempt to guess its height.

The blood-red stuff of it shone like metal. There was a lofty frame of colossal beams and girders There were moving parts, so intricate, so strange, that he could readily find no name or explanation for them. In particular, his eye was caught by a vast, shimmering white object, shaped like a flattened orange, that moved irregularly up and down between two colossal plates of crimson. The whole was enclosed in a transparent greenish dome, that seemed somehow akin to the sky.

Despair took hold of him.

'Against the scale of that machine,' he muttered, 'we're no more than five flies.'

They plodded on. In the pellucid atmosphere, the machine always looked almost near enough to touch. And always it retreated, mockingly at their weary efforts. At last, at the plaintive insistence of Giles Habibula, they halted. The *Halcyon Bird* was lost to view. They huddled in a lonely little circle by the sledges, on that shimmering vastness. They drank, ate sparingly, and tried to rest.

There was no wind. The cool air was oppressively still. The green sky did not change. There were no clouds.

'The planet doesn't rotate.' Jay Kalam commented. 'There is no weather, nor even any time. It is a world without change.'

A terrible silence overhung them. Nothing lived or moved or gave voice upon all the empty plain. The green sky was equally devoid of life or motion. The cold disc of the purple sun hung steady, high above the straight horizon. They could see the glowing lines of the triple beam, converging toward it. The multitudinous planets of the swarm stood motionless in the pale green void. They neither rotated nor changed position.

131

Giles Habibula wiped sweat from his yellow brow with the back of his hand.

'Ah, me!' he moaned. 'A fearful world to die in! Upon one journey of forlorn hope, old Giles carried a bottle of wine through the mortal hardship of a continent larger than the precious Earth. But then he fought enemies he could understand. He never felt such need of the bright strength of wine.' He fumbled in the packs on the sledges, and found a bottle of some rare vintage from the asteroid. Watching with a jealous eye, he offered it to each of the others in turn, and at last drained it gratefully.

Even Jay Kalam was worn to confessing despondency.

'It's true,' he agreed bleakly 'that things were never quite so bad for us, not even on the Runaway Star. Though the things we fought then were able scientists and terrible foes, they were still defeated refugees from their own environment.

'But the Cometeers have conquered theirs. The creatures of the Runaway Star were things that we could sometimes kill, but the Cometeers aren't flesh.' His thin lips set. 'I doubt very much that any weapon men ever made could destroy one of them.'

Startled, Hal Samdu peered at him. 'Not even Aladoree's ?'

He shook his head. 'AKKA will destroy anything material – but I'm not certain that the Cometeers are material at all.'

'Ah, so, Jay,' croaked Giles Habibula. 'Our plight is desperate. In seeking to balk the Cometeers and destroy Stephen Orco, we are no more than five ants making war on all the System –'

His voice wheezed into silence. His dull eyes, staring into the green sky, seemed to film. The breath went out of him.

'A good thing!' he gasped. 'A good thing we drank the wine.'

Bob Star saw a distant object, skimming swiftly toward them through the green. It came from the direction of the *Halcyon Bird*. Jay Kalam caught at Giles Habibula's arm, as he started away.

'Don't run,' he said. 'There's nowhere to go. If we crouch down, perhaps they won't see us.'

Bob Star was huddled beside Kay Nymidee. He caught her hand, and it closed upon his with a desperate pressure. Her face was drawn, white with strain. Her pale lips quivered. Overwhelming terror shuddered in her eyes. Pity for her stabbed him like a blade.

A nerve-severing sound tore him away from the girl. He jumped, startled, terrified. For a moment he could not identify the sound. Then he knew that it had been Giles Habibula's scream. Now the old man was trembling, sinking slowly backward upon his knees. His moon face was yellow-grey, contorted with dread. His small round eyes were fixed, glazed, bulging.

'What is it, Giles?'

'Mortal me!' the old man sobbed. 'It's the fearful thing – or another like it – that ate Mark Lardo!'

Bob Star looked up then, and found the object he had glimpsed a moment ago in the far distance, now already upon them. For the first time, his horror-filmed eyes rested upon one of the Cometeers.

It was hanging in the air, close beside them.

Floating low was a tiny star of red, veiled in a misty crimson moon. Ten feet above it hung a violet star, wrapped in violet fog. The red seemed hot as the core of a sun, and the violet as cold as outermost space.

A mist swirled between the moons. There was life in its motion; it was like a throbbing artery of light. Red star and violet star beat like hearts of fire. Girdling the misty pillar was a wide green ring. It was the only part of the creature that looked at all substantial – and even it, Bob Star knew, could pass through the hard alloys of a space cruiser's hull.

His dazed mind first received the thing with startled incredulity. He blinked, and looked down at the dark plain, and rubbed his eyes. But the thing had not gone, when he looked again. And its hideous reality ate into his mind, like a corrosive poison. He fought the queer, numbing horror that came flooding from it.

133

'Just coloured lights,' he muttered. 'Moving mist.' 'Shouldn't be afraid–'

But mind-killing dread swept into him. His numbed senses perceived a terrible entity within, beyond, those coloured lights; an alien mind, supernally powerful and completely evil. Every atom of his body reacted to it with automatic, shocked revulsion.

And the incessant beat of that old, strange pain, behind the triangular scar of the Iron Confessor, was suddenly redoubled. Every throb of it became a sickening, staggering blow against the naked tissues of his brain.

He braced himself against fear and pain. Swiftly, half unconsciously, his fingers had been slipping fresh cells into his two proton pistols. The two weapons came up, now, together.

The emerald ring looked to be the most material part of blast. Those two blinding swords of violet ruin would have the being. He pointed the guns at that, and pulled the firing levers all the way, to exhaust the cells in one single cut through a solid foot of tempered steel. They would have electrocuted any living being – as the System knew life – at the distance of a mile.

But, like phantom swords, they flashed through the green ring, harmless.

Quivering to the shocking of icy dismay, Bob Star recalled Jay Kalam's opinion that no human weapon could injure the Cometeers.

'Kay–' despair rasped from his leathery throat, 'Kay–'

His voice stopped, as if to the touch of death. For out of the pillar of swirling light another voice had spoken, whose careless, mocking levity was the most appalling thing Bob Star had ever heard.

'That's rather useless, Bob.' It was the voice of Stephen Orco.

Bob Star staggered backward. That light, ringing voice was more terrible than all the shining horror in the air.

'You had your chance, Bob,' said the voice. 'When I was in prison on Neptune, you had only to touch a little red button. But you failed. I'm afraid you'll never succeed. For now, Bob, I've a body that cannot be destroyed.'

'You –' dread drew his tone to a quivering edge. 'You're *that*?'

'I am what you see, Bob. One of the drivers of the comet.'

A low, mocking chuckle rang inside the shining being. There was a little silence, and then the clear voice spoke again:

'Perhaps, Bob,' it suggested lightly, 'you would be glad to hear of your mother? It must be some time since you left her.'

Bob Star leaned forward, sick and trembling. A gloating satisfaction in that careless voice cleft his spine like a cold axe. Hoarsely, through stiff, unwilling lips, he forced the whisper: 'What about her?'

'I was alarmed for your mother, Bob,' the liquid mockery of Stephen Orco's voice flowed on. 'For she has been lost. My new associates searched the System for her, in vain. I was somewhat worried, for her life is the only barrier before me, now.

'But her capture has just been reported to me. It appears that your father, on his *Phantom Star*, was taking her away from the System, toward the star 61 Cygni. My associates have overtaken them. And I hope soon, Bob, to meet your mother, here within the comet.'

Chapter Fifteen

THE CATTLE AND THE HERDSMEN

Bob Star woke from a singular dream.

In the dream he had thought that his body had been exchanged for the shining form of one of the Cometeers. And this bodiless entity, himself, was flying through the green vacancy of the comet's interior. Ahead of him, fleeing in a similar shining guise, was Stephen Orco.

This Stephen Orco, of the dream, was carrying away a woman. He was going to consume her, in some dreadful way. Only a shrunken husk would be left, bleached, wrinkled, hideous. And even the whimpering husk would die, and crumble to the iridescent ash and fluid. Sometimes the woman was his mother, and sometimes she was golden-eyed Kay Nymidee.

Somehow, even in his bodiless form, Bob Star carried a weapon. He had no picture of its shape, but it was something that could destroy Stephen Orco, and save the changing woman. But a terrible fear was beating him down, out of the green abysm. His shining shape was reeling under the incessant blows of a great red hammer of pain. Stephen Orco's voice was shouting furiously at him, turned to agony by the cruel mechanism of the Iron Confessor:

'You can't! You can't kill anybody!'

He woke, and knew that it was the low, anxious voice of Kay Nymidee that had roused him.

'*Sa daspete!*' she was urging. '*Sa daspete!*'

He was lying down, with his head on her knees. Her hands were cool on his forehead, and they seemed to soothe the old pain behind the scar. He looked up, to find her anxious face oddly blurred and strange beneath pale green light. He tried to rise, and discovered the numbness of his body. Hideous as his dream had been, recollection came back. Ringing in his brain, he heard again the lightly mocking voice of Stephen Orco.

'I'm not going to hasten your destruction, Bob. A ship has been ordered here, to pick you up and your companions. You will be taken, along with a load of the prisoners from Pluto, down into this fortress of my new companions. And ultimately –'

A chuckle had come from that shining thing.

'Have you ever seen the way we feed, Bob?' that bright voice murmured. 'Well, you're going to. But while you're waiting for that, there's something else I want you to think about.

'I can't be killed.

'You've already proved that, with your own guns. And it's no use clenching your fists and shaking your head – your face confesses your reluctant admiration of my new physical equipment. Certainly, it's admirable enough. Space is no barrier to me now, neither is any material wall. But its best feature is immortality.

'My new body is truly eternal, Bob. It has mass and potential energy. But its mass is in no form you know as matter, Bob, and its energy is beyond the comprehension of your physics. Not even your mother's weapon could destroy it.

'These deathless dwellings for intelligence are the supreme achievements of my new associates, Bob. You had not guessed that they were artificial? But the drivers of the comet once were beings of flesh. Not far different, perhaps, from mankind. But they became impatient with frailty, incapacity, death. They called upon their high science for a means of transferring their minds to eternal constructs of specialized energy.

'The Cometeers agreed to make me one of their number, to secure themselves from your mother's weapon – AKKA could destroy all their somewhat elaborate equipment and possessions of course, even though it could not directly annihilate their bodies.

'And now, Bob,' the gay voice mocked him. 'I shall be forced to leave you. Your parents, as I told you, are being brought into the comet. I must go to welcome your mother.'

Stephen Orco chuckled at the mute agony twisting Bob Star's face.

'I wish to discuss with her the principle of AKKA. There are points not clear from my own research. And when our discussions are ended, Bob –

'If you wonder why we must feed the way we do – it's because even these indestructible devices of life are incomplete. They were designed to be eternal vehicles for intelligence, and they can preserve our minds forever, against all possible assaults. Yet their very perfection becomes almost a flaw.

'Because they aren't the bodies we used to own. Their senses are superior, but not the same. The mechanisms of emotion were largely omitted from their design, as useless heritages of the flesh. The consequent penalty we must pay for our undying perfection is a periodic hunger for the emotions and sensations we have lost.

'With their usual ingenuity, however, my new friends have found a way to satisfy that hunger. The vital energy of our immortal mechanisms requires occasional renewal, from the transmutation of ordinary matter. By taking that matter from bodies like we used to own, in a way that stimulates the most intense emotion and sensation, we are able to satisfy both those recurrent appetites – the physical and the spritual, so to speak – at the same time.

'Since our minds came from a number of vastly different races, we must each keep our own herds of the proper creatures. I am arranging to maintain a human colony, Bob – you and your companions will presently see the arrangements.

'I'm planning, however, to make my first meal upon your mother. I understand from my new friends that the close rapport. of mind and emotion set up during the feeding process will enable me to pick her thoughts of all I want to know. And then –'

The shining thing chuckled softly.

'Have you seen what is left, after one of us has eaten, Bob? Can you see your mother, so? Small as a child, shrivelled and colourless, whimpering for death? When you do see that, Bob, I've a question for you. I'm going to ask you if the nameless castaway of space hasn't matched the pampered darling of the Purple Hall.'

The sardonic voice had faded then, as green mists thickened to veil the Cometeer . . .

Bob Star moved uncertainly again, fighting the lingering stiffness of that paralysis, and Kay Nymidee helped him to sit up. Blinking to clear his eyes, he saw that heatless purple sun in the green sky again, and the slick blue flatness of the master planet. The two improvised sledges lay close beside him. Jay Kalam and Hal Samdu and Giles Habibula were unpacking them hastily, flinging aside the spare proton guns and extra cells they had carried.

'Ah, so,' he heard Giles Habibula wheeze mournfully. 'The monster ruined them, every one, the way that other did my precious geodynes aboard the *Halcyon Bird*.' He saw Bob Star, and brightened. 'Ah, lad, old Giles is glad to see you up again. We thought you would never wake –'

'There!' Hal Samdu was rumbling. 'It must be the ship he said was coming for us.'

Lurching stiffly to his feet, Bob Star peered into the green sky.

He saw a flying thing, slanting down toward them. It was a thick, horizontal saucer-shape, red as that colossal machine standing above the blue horizon. Its upper face formed a deck, which ringed a low red dome. It came with no roar of rockets, nor any visible means of propulsion.

Bob Star caught apprehensively at Jay Kalam's arm.

'What –' he whispered hoarsely, 'what can we do?'

'Nothing, but try to preserve our lives,' said the weary-voiced commander. 'And watch for some chance – some miracle of fate – for so long as we live –'

The red disc came down gently, at some little distance.

139

The deceptive conditions made distance and size difficult to estimate, but it suddenly looked much larger than Bob Star had first supposed it.

The clang of some metal thing – perhaps the cover of a hatch – jarred Bob Star, even in his hopeless apathy. He heard raucous hoots, and answering reverberations that were like the booming of great drums. These were the same uncanny sounds, he realized, that he had heard from the invisible ship which carried Stephen Orco away from Neptune. A great, square opening gasped suddenly black in the crimson side of the disc. A square door had fallen outward, to form an inclined gangway. Marching down that incline came monstrous things.

No longer – despite the unsolved enigma of Kay Nymidee's humanity – did Bob Star expect to find beings like men within the comet. Yet he was not prepared for the mind-shaking impact of the things that came down the gangway.

There were eight, of three different sorts.

The foremost was a ten-foot sphere of some silvery metal, surrounded with a dark equatorial band. At first Bob Star thought that it was rolling; then he saw that only the band turned, sliding about the globe. Each pole was a dark, glittering bulge, that looked like a faceted eye. About each bulge were spaced three long, gleaming metallic tentacles, now coiled close to the hemispheres.

The two creatures behind were slender cones in shape, nearly twenty feet tall. They were bright green; their skins had an oily lustre. Their bases, apparently, were elastic, inflated membranes, expanded to hemispheres, upon which they bounded forward with a curious, astounding agility. The slender upper parts of the cones were flexible necks. The dark, pointed organs that tipped them turned this way and that, like singular heads. Green cones bouncing upon pneumatic cushions – they looked like grotesque nursery toys, but there was nothing toy-like about their air of deadly purpose.

The remaining five were slender tripedal giants. Their

lean bodies, vaguely suggestive of the human, stood perhaps fifteen feet tall. They were covered with a dully glistening, dark-red armour, like the chitin of gigantic insects. Each had six slender upper limbs, forming a kind of fringe about a cluster of stalked organs, where the head should have been. They carried a kind of harness slung with a variety of curious implements or weapons.

'Mortal me!' gasped Giles Habibula. 'Are these fearful things the lords of the comet? And not the shining monsters?'

'I don't think so.' The commander stood gravely watching their approach. 'I imagine these are the slaves of the Cometeers. Herdsmen, perhaps, of the things they breed for food –'

He fell abruptly silent.

The white sphere turned a little aside, a few yards away. It halted, resting on the dark belt. Hoarse, raucous hoots came from it – like commands. The green cones answered, with dull booming reverberation that seemed to come from their inflated pedal membranes. The scarlet, three-legged creatures made no sound. But they came on with the cones, spreading out as if to encircle the five by the sledges. Bob Star broke at last out of his trance of horror, reaching automatically for his proton guns.

'Wait, Bob,' Jay Kalam muttered wearily. 'Our weapons have all been ruined. We can't resist –'

'But Jay –' protested Hal Samdu, 'we can't give up – without a fight!'

'We must,' Jay Kalam insisted quietly. 'We must preserve our lives, and hope for some opportunity –'

The giant made a mute, hurt sound.

'Surrender?' he rumbled incredulously. 'Legionnaires don't surrender!' Catching up a dead proton pistol, like a club, he strode out to meet the nearest bounding green cone. 'We can't give up,' his voice came back. 'Not with Aladoree still in danger –'

Kay Nymidee ran after him, as if to catch his arm, calling urgently.

'*Pahratee!*'

She was too late. The thin, flexible upright tip of the green cone whipped over toward him. From the dark, tapered organ at the tip of it, which was like a pointed head, there flashed a thin and blinding ray of orange light.

Hal Samdu crumpled down, groaning with helpless agony.

'We can't resist,' Jay Kalam repeated hopelessly. 'Help me carry him, Bob. We'll go aboard – if that's what they want. There's nothing –'

His quiet voice broke off, with a breathless exclamation. And Bob Star was amazed when he turned and spoke to Kay Nymidee, with strange words as soft and liquid-toned as her own.

The prison-hold filled nearly all the lowest level of the disc-ship. The vast circle of it, some five hundred feet across, was broken only by a doorless wall, perhaps enclosing the engine rooms, which shut off a part of the centre. There were no ports, and the only light was a dim red glare reflected from the high metal ceiling. The ventilation was bad, sanitary conveniences were few, and the hold reeked with the odours of its occupants.

The entrance was a massive grille of red metal bars, at the top of a long ramp. One of the white spheres remained on guard beyond the grille, but none of the cometary beings came into the hold.

The five new prisoners were pushed through the door, and left upon the ramp. Examining Hal Samdu, who was still unable to speak or to sit up, Bob Star and Giles Habibula found a small, circular inflamed patch on his temple.

Bob Star and Jay Kalam had attempted to carry him as they came aboard, but one of the thin red giants had taken the limp body from them, in its fringe of clustered arms. And they had meekly followed.

The miserable thousands imprisoned in the hold were mostly sitting or lying on the bare metal floor. They were clad in haphazard fragments of clothing; only a few had odd little bundles of their possessions. Their unwashed faces were haggard with fatigue and despair, and the sound that rose up from all of them was a weary murmur of hopeless apathy, without any light or laughter.

On the ramp, Bob Star was accosted by a gaunt, grey-faced man who had been stalking like a tired spectre, across the great floor, stepping over recumbent bodies to look at the face of every slumbering or weeping child.

'Have you seen my son?' the weary stranger rasped. 'A blue-eyed lad, with curly yellow hair. His name is John – after the great John Star. Have you seen him?'

Bob Star shook his head, and saw hope extinguished by despair.

'Where do you come from?' he asked.

'From Plut.' The blood-shot eyes looked at him with a dull curiosity. 'My name is Hector Valdin. I was a worker in the platinum mines of Votanga.' His gnarled hands made a heavy gesture. 'These people – they were my friends and neighbours there. But now –'

'What brought you here?'

'Don't you know?' The gaunt man peered at him. 'Well, they say something happened to all the Legion bases. I met a man who saw the end of Fort Votanga. The batteries began to fire – and stopped. A red light shone down on the walls – and they crumbled away. There was only a great pit left.'

The weary man shrugged vaguely.

'I don't know what that was. But a green thing began growing in the sky. It was a comet, men said. And Pluto was being dragged inside it, somehow. I don't know –'

His teeth ground together in sudden, savage pain.

'But then these monsters came. They burned our houses, to drive out our women and children, so that they could catch them. They're taking us somewhere. I don't know where. But my son John is lost.' The red eyes came pleadingly back to Bob Star's face. 'You haven't seen a little blue-eyed lad –'

So this, Bob Star thought bitterly, was to be the fate of all humanity.

'Do the creatures ever come in here?' His question came of some vague and hopeless impulse toward escape. 'Do they ever open that door?'

'They never come among us.' Hector Valdin shook his head. 'The door hasn't been opened since we were herded into the vessel – save to admit you.'

'How do they clean the floor, and feed the prisoners.'

'They don't clean the floor,' Hector Valdin said. 'And the only food they give us is a sour slop that runs into troughs by the wall.'

The hopeless eyes searched Bob Star again, with a weary wonderment.

'Where was your home?' he asked. 'I think I never saw you in Votanga.'

Bob Star had looked away from him, across the hopeless murmuring misery of the thousands sitting and lying on the floor, and then back at the massive locked grating at the top of the ramp.

'It doesn't matter, if you don't feel like talking.' Hector Valdin shrugged. 'Most of us are still too dazed to know just what happened.' He straightened wearily. 'Anyhow, friend, I must go on now, to look for my son, John –'

A sudden blue light had come into Bob Star's eyes. And a smile had come over his thin face, a hard and dangerous smile.

'Wait, Hector Valdin!' His voice had a bright and eager ring. 'I'll tell you who we are, and how we came to be here.'

'Never mind,' the gaunt man muttered. 'It doesn't really matter. I just find John –'

'Wait!' Bob Star called urgently. 'If you honour the name of John Star –'

And Hector Valdin came back, with a little of the leaden apathy already lifted from his face. And others, near at hand, gathered around them to listen. For Bob Star's voice rang strong with an urgent, compelling eagerness. And he spoke magic names, from the glorious history of man.

'. . . Jay Kalam, who is commander of the Legion . . . The

big man, just sitting up, is Hal Samdu, who went with my father and the others out to the Runaway Star . . . Giles Habibula – he can open that door, to let us out into that ship! My mother, the keeper of the peace. She is a prisoner, now, about to be murdered . . .'

Bob Star talked on. He groped for stirring words. He was a little surprised at the confidence, the ringing strength, in his voice. For in his heart he knew there was no hope, He knew they were all cattle for the Cometeers.

He knew that Stephen Orco could not be killed.

Yet soon many men were listening to him. A quick interest was penetrating the leaden despair upon their weary faces. And the bright finger of hope transfigured now one and now another –

Chapter Sixteen

JOHN STAR'S SON

The first conversation of Jay Kalam and Kay Nymidee was curiously hard to interrupt. It had begun, out upon the jewel-smooth armour of the planet, when the girl called out for Hal Samdu to stop, and the surprised commander addressed her in her own language.

Even in the presence of their captors, her face shone with sudden delight. She ran joyously to the commander, and threw her slim arms about him. She lifted on tiptoe to kiss both his lean cheeks. Then, almost ignoring the creatures herding them into the ship, she was talking at him furiously. And Jay Kalam replied awkwardly, haltingly, but as if he understood.

They scarcely paused when their captors pushed them down into the prison-hold, and locked the massive grate behind them. On the ramp inside, they kept on talking. Kay Nymidee spoke very fast. Her white face showed a great play of expression, smiling with joy, frowning with the effort of making her meaning clear; it was bright with hope, shadowed again with apprehension.

Jay Kalam's dark face, in contrast, was intently fixed. For the most part he merely listened, his dark brow furrowed with the effort of comprehension. But frequently he broke in, to beg the girl to repeat, or to ask some halting question.

Bob Star came to them more than once, and went away again when they gave him no attention. Men were following him, now, led by words like golden banners blowing. That still amazed him, for he was only a boy, afraid, half disabled from a strange and ancient injury. But they did, and he went on, rejoicing in the magic of those words.

146

Kay Nymidee came running to him at last. She called something and seemed hurt again because he didn't understand.

'She's asking,' Jay Kalam said, 'if you know Spanish.'

'Spanish?'

'Yes. That's her language"

'Spanish? How does she know Spanish?' He was bewildered. 'Isn't she a native of the comet?'

'Kay is,' the commander said. 'But her race isn't. I told you how improbable –'

'How does that happen? How did her people get into the comet?'

'An odd story.' Jay Kalam stroked at the dark angle of his jaw. 'But credible enough, with what we know of the Cometeers. The bare facts are all she has been able to tell me. Kay's Spanish, you see, and mine are almost two different languages. Mine is due to an interest in the plays of Lope de Vega, who wrote fourteen hundred years ago. Hers is the Spanish of a thousand years later, still farther changed by four hundred years of adaptation to an alien environment. Her accent is so unfamiliar that it is the merest accident that I recognized her tongue at all – when she told Hal Samdu to stop. And her scientific words, of course, are nearly all totally unfamiliar. That makes her message peculiarly difficult to understand.'

'Four hundred years?' Bob Star gaped at him. 'Have the Cometeers been here before?'

Jay Kalam shook his head, explaining:

'You may recall, Bob, from your history books, that during the latter part of the twenty-sixth century the Andean Republic passed through a brief golden age. For a few years, in science and nearly all the arts, as well as in wealth and military power, it was the leading nation of Earth.

'The climax of that splendid era was the *Conquistador* expedition. In the greatest geodesic cruiser that had ever been built, a hundred men and women left Santiago upon what was planned to be the System's greatest voyage of science and exploration.

'The *Conquistador* never returned.

'The hundred had been the intellectual flower of the republic. Their loss may have been the blow that broke the golden age, because the northern lands soon resumed their supremacy, and Spanish is now almost a dead language.'

'The *Conquistador* – ?'

'It was captured by the Cometeers,' Jay Kalam said. 'Apparently their ships were continually sent ahead, at velocities far beyond the speed of light, on scouting expeditions – I suppose in search of planetary systems worth raiding.

'Such an invisible scout met the *Conquistador*, somewhere beyond Pluto. Her entire crew was carried back to the comet, which was then some hundreds of light-years away.

Many of the prisoners were kept alive, and eventually a few of them escaped. Aided by other enslaved beings, they got away from the master planet, in a captured ship, and reached one of the outlying planets of the cluster.

'For two generations they existed as miserable fugitives, until the survivors found their way into a great cavern, learned the plans of the Cometeers and they determined to warn and aid the System. Kay Nymidee is their daughter – after four hundred years.

'They made scientific progress. The projector that brought Kay to the asteroid is their most brilliant achievement. I don't entirely understand her explanation, but apparently it operates by warping space-time to bring two remote points so close together that light – or even, finally, a material body – can cross the gap.

'The machine, anyhow, was developed by Kay's father. And he had been using it to send Kay into the secret places of the Cometeers, after their secrets. They detected it when she was trying to warn you, on Neptune. They raided the cavern. Kay is the only one who escaped. At the last moment, her father used the machine to send her to you, upon the asteroid.'

Bob Star caught eagerly at his arm.

'What has she been trying to tell us?' he gasped abruptly. 'About Stephen Orco and the Cometeers?'

'The Cometeers can be destroyed,' Jay Kalam said. 'But Kay doesn't know how. She knows only that the means exist. She says the Cometeers are ordinarily immortal. But their rulers possess some secret agency that can destroy them – something invented by the ancient designers of their artificial bodies. She has no idea what it is, but she does know where the secret is kept.'

'Where?'

'In a fortress deep inside this planet – you remember Kay's drawing?'

Breathless and trembling, Bob Star nodded.

'Well, this planet is a world truly dead – cold to the centre. It is honeycombed with cavernous hollows, as we might have suspected from its low mean density. The chief stronghold of the Cometeers, where they guard that secret, is down somewhere near the centre of the planet. Kay has been trying to guide us to it.'

Bob Star stood frowning at the grave commander, his brief hope already crumbling.

'The information is very useful now!' he muttered bitterly. 'When we are prisoners, unarmed and condemned! When the weapon that can kill Stephen Orco is hidden in the middle of an armoured planet, fifteen thousand miles beneath us, and guarded with all the science of the Cometeers!'

Bob Star was never satisfied with his part in the rebellion of the prisoners. True, the plan of action – if anything so vague, so wild, so desperately hopeless could be called a plan – was his. And it was he, at last, who led the rush from the hold.

But those five mad seconds never contented him.

Hector Valdin had gone with him through the weary apathy of the prison-hold. He had introduced Bob Star to his fellow miners, his old neighbours, simply as John Star's

149

son. And Bob Star had touched them with the greatness of
the System, the old glory of mankind. He stirred them with
the great names of John Star and Commander Kalam; of
Hal Samdu and Giles Habibula; of Aladoree, the beloved
keeper of the peace. They rose to follow the bugle of those
names.

And Bob Star had come at last to Giles Habibula, de-
manding: 'Giles, can you open the door?'

'Why lad?' The old man started. The yellow moon of
his face went ashen. 'In the precious name of life, why
should I open the door?'

'Can you?' Bob insisted.

'That monstrous globe is watching,' whispered the old
man. 'And there are fearful hordes above –'

'But can you?'

'Ah, the sad fate of genius!' He shook his head, dolefully.
'Yes, lad, I can open the door. I watched the working
of the lock as they let us in, and I've been looking at the
thing for hours since, until I can see every part within the
case. It's a combination affair, with discs and tumblers,
worked by sliding rods. The design is good – though not
good enough to baffle poor old Giles Habibula. But
why—?'

Jay Kalam, with whom Bob Star had discussed the piece
of reckless audacity he called a plan, said soberly: 'Do it,
Giles.'

'Not yet!' The old man shuddered. 'Not beneath the
eye of that fearful globe –'

'We'll try to distract it,' Bob Star promised.

He made a sign to the gaunt, grey-faced miner. Hector
Valdin lunged toward Kay Nymidee, grasping for her, as
they had planned. She screamed, stumbling toward Bob
Star. Bob Star swung at his haggard ally. Others rushed to
circle them. A noisy riot swept up and down the ramp.

Meanwhile, Giles Habibula crept trembling to the massive
lock at the top of the ramp. Shouting, Jay Kalam was
pushing his way towards the centre of the milling throng.
And gigantic Hal Samdu was fighting now, with such a

grim and silent earnestness as if he forgot it was make-believe. And Giles Habibula came lumbering at last down the ramp, gasping for Bob Star. His face was yellow-green, glistening with sweat.

'Lad!' he wheezed. 'Lad, the door is unlocked. You may go through, if you are such a fool –'

Bob Star led the cheering mob up the ramp. He reached the massive red grating, and his clear voice called a ringing command. Magically, then, the mob became a terrible and desperate army. Hal Samdu and Hector Valdin helped him fling aside the unlocked grating. And he led the rush upon the white sphere beyond, to pit bare human flesh against its metal might.

It was a mad thing; Jay Kalam had made him see that. These thousands behind him were weaponless, already once beaten. Even if they took the ship, they were far indeed from the well-guarded secret that could kill Stephen Orco.

But Bob Star led his crush of silent, empty-handed men against the metal sphere. They lifted it, and surged with it toward the red wall of the corridor. It was hooting a raucous alarm; and the white tentacles seized the bodies of men, to beat men down with living flails.

Others took the place of the fallen. Bob Star had made death itself a victory to the men behind him. And a supernal thing strode among the prisoners as they marched from the hold, something greater than any man. It was that intangible, ineffable power that touched a few beasts in the wilderness of early Earth, and created the unity that is mankind and the glory of the far-flung System.

It was that something, transfiguring human flesh, that smashed the hooting sphere against the red metal wall, again and again, until the faceted eyes were shattered, and its surface was crushed in, until the deadly tentacles were still and the hooting ceased – and then tore it into fragments, to make weapons.

That same power led the ragged horde down the corridor, to meet the guard: Another argent sphere, hooting hoarse commands. Three of the tall green cones, bouncing upon distended bases, booming their threats, flashing orange-red rays from their narrow, pointed heads. A full score of the red-armoured, three-legged giants, with strange colours flashing from the stalked organs where their heads should have been, their tentacular limbs clutching golden weapons.

It was hopeless, as Jay Kalam had warned. It was useless, utter folly . . .

But that supernal power would not be stopped. Bob Star led the way to meet that alien band, shouting, flourishing one of the tentacles of the dismembered globe, which had stiffened now into a silver spear. A great voice rolled up behind him.

That, for Bob Star, was the end of the battle.

He had flung his argent spear at one of the green, bounding cones. He saw it strike the oily, glistening skin, and sink deep. He plunged forward, to grasp it and strike again. But he saw the green neck flex, so that the narrow head pointed at him; he saw the beginning of an orange flash.

Then a red and merciless spear of pain drove through the pale old scar on his forehead, and thrust deep into his brain. Red agony exploded through his skull, and faded slowly into darkness. Faintly, as his sick consciousness went out like a dying flame, he heard the thundering, triumphant shout:

'Take the ship!'

Chapter Seventeen

THE HUMAN ROCKET

Bob Star woke once more from the same strange dream.

Again his body had been the shining, weightless body of one of the Cometeers. And again he was pursuing the eternal, supernal form of Stephen Orco, who fled with a woman – his mother, sometimes, and sometimes Kay Nymidee. Once more he had been crushed down by a great hammer of red pain, and overwhelmed by the old fear that yelled:

'You can't – You can't kill –'

His trembling hand was pressed against his forehead, when he woke. There, above that old scar, the skin felt swollen and painful to his fingers – where that organic ray had struck him. The old agony still throbbed beneath it, as if the three-edged blade of the Iron Confessor still stabbed intermittently into his brain.

Awake, he still felt as strangely weightless as he had been in that dream. He found that he was floating in the air, and the lack of gravitation made him giddily uncomfortable. He had to swallow a sudden sense of panic, when he found no support beneath him. Groping desperately for something substantial, he looked around him blankly.

Around him were the hard blue walls of a shaft or pit, perhaps fifty feet square and a hundred deep – too large a chamber, he decided, to be part of the prison-ship. After a moment of twisting and peering, he discovered his old companions.

Giles Habibula was clinging to what seemed the bottom of the pit, where a circle of slender rods of red metal projected from the polished wall. His deft, sensitive fingers were sliding the rods in and out, twisting them; the yellow globe of his head was cocked as if to listen.

Jay Kalam and Kay Nymidee were near him, equally weightless, busy with some unfamiliar instrument. From a rectangular case of red metal they were taking wires and coils and odd-looking parts of scarlet metal, and little round black cells.

It took him a moment longer to locate Hal Samdu. Bruised somewhat, covered with blood-stained bandages, the giant was clinging to the edge of the pit, peering out as if on guard. One great hand clutched a long rod of yellow metal – a weapon, Bob Star knew, that must have been taken from one of the lean, red-armoured beings.

Beyond him, beyond the square mouth of the pit, yawned a dark, cavernous abysm. Far distant in it he could glimpse rugged walls of dark rock, and part of a machine that must have been fantastically huge, faintly illuminated with a ghastly crimson light.

A curious sickness came upon Bob Star as he tried to move, as if every tissue of his body clamoured for the certainty and the orientation of weight. Yearning, for something to cling to, he floundered about in the air until his foot kicked the wall.

The action had surprising results. It sent him hurtling, head foremost, across the fifty feet to the opposite wall. Dismayed, he flung out his arms to fend for his head. The undue force of the gesture sent him spinning back across the pit. Giles Habibula reached away from the circle of rods, to catch his ankle.

'Better cling to this bit of rail, lad,' he advised absently. 'Or you'll be smashing out your wits, before you ever get them back. For we're almost at the centre of this fearful planet, and nearly free of gravity. One step could carry you a mile –'

'At the centre of the planet?' He shook himself dazedly. 'Tell me, Giles –'

The old man had returned to his business of twisting and sliding the scarlet rods.

'Ah, lad,' he wheezed, abstractedly, 'you've been out for a mortal long time – the ray from that creature struck your old wound; I think it almost killed you.'

'The ship?' Bob Star asked eagerly. 'Did we take the ship?'

'Ah, so, we took the ship.' He slid the rods in and out, listening with his ear against the case. 'Thanks to the mad courage you had put into the prisoners, lad – they overwhelmed our guards like a wild sea. Aided, too, by the unrewarded genius of a poor old soldier in the Legion. And by the miner, Hector Valdin; he led them on – until he died.'

The absent voice had faded, and Bob Star asked:

'If we're at the centre of the planet, how did we get here?'

'We were already in the cavernous space outside, when we took the ship,' said Giles Habibula. 'The core of the planet is a hive of the Cometeers and their cattle.'

He shuddered, but oddly his thick fingers didn't seem to pause or tremble.

'When the ship was ours,' he went on, 'Jay and the lass took command. They disembarked us here, an hour ago. Our comrades went on with the ship, to seek some refuge in the caverns. Ever since, I've been toiling with this lock.

'It's nothing simple! The number of possible combinations would make your head spin, lad. To open it by trial and error would take from now until the sun grows cold. Ah, me! the Cometeers are clever –

'But the lass bade me open it, lad. She says their inner stronghold is somewhere beyond, where they guard the weapon that we must take.'

Bob Star nodded – and bit his lip. 'I'm sorry, if my talk has bothered you –'

'Not so, lad,' protested the old man. 'Talk but oils the working of my precious genius. But this lock is a fearful test for it. Never was such a riddle built into cold metal, lad. And never was old Giles so unfit to draw out the answer. For he's ill, lad. The stark hand of death is close upon him.'

But his fingers didn't cease their labour. Bob Star glanced at Jay Kalam and Kay Nymidee, who still were busy over the intricate thing in the red metal case.

'What's that?'

'Some blessed contraption Jay tore out of the control room of the ship, before we came off. From the wonderment on his face, I doubt that he knows himself what it is.'

Bob Star was about to let go the rail he held, to try to reach them, when a sudden, unendurable sickness seized him. Here, near the planet's heart, he had no weight. Directions had no meaning. His surroundings had begun to spin, dizzily. At one moment, the blue shaft was horizontal. The next, it was an inverted pit, and he was clinging precariously to the roof of a vertiginous abyss.

Giles Habibula, beside him, was doubled up again, his moon face greenish, sweat-beaded.

'Jay!' he gasped hoarsely. 'I'm sick – deathly ill! The wine we found on that asteroid – I think it was poisoned! I'm dying, Jay. Dying –'

'Not yet, Giles,' Jay Kalam called. 'We all feel upset, from being without weight. It is the same as the space sickness they used to have on the old rocket fliers, before the invention of the gravity cell. Some people are almost immune, as I am. Others never become adjusted to it.

'Anyhow, Giles, you must open the lock. All we have done is useless, unless we get through this door.'

'I can't do it, Jay!' The old man was sweating and panting. 'I'm too mortal ill. The torture of a dying body destroys my concentration. For life's sake, Jay –'

'You must, Giles. For the keeper of the peace!'

Giles Habibula sighed, and bent again to his task.

'Ah,' he sobbed. 'Genius draws a bitter lot –'

Kay Nymidee was still busy over the red metal case. Now Bob Star heard her utter a little cry of satisfaction. She held up a dark, opalescent prism, and swiftly explained something to Jay Kalam. He nodded gravely, and rapidly they began to reassemble the mysterious device.

A dull, coughing explosion drew Bob Star's eyes to the square mouth of the pit. Pale smoke had puffed from Hal Samdu's captured weapon. Beyond, he saw a white globe approaching. It came sailing through the air, black belt spinning, crystal eyes glittering, white tentacles sprawling. In the midst of his consternation, Bob Star found time to wonder briefly if it were all machine, or if it contained a living brain.

He heard its abrupt, hoarse hoot of alarm, close on the explosion. Hal Samdu fumbled a moment with the golden weapon. Then he hurled it spinning toward the silver globe, and came plunging down the shaft, to sprawl against the bottom of it.

'Aye, Jay!' he rumbled apprehensively. 'We are discovered. A horde of the monsters coming. I destroyed one – but the golden gun would not work again –'

His voice stilled to a terrific vibration that thundered down the shaft. It was the clang of a huge gong, deep as the note of a hammered planet. And suddenly, beyond the silver sphere, an alien horde was following into the pit: huge green cones, and red, grotesque giants in golden harness. Another globe brought up the rear.

They were swimming through the air.

Bob Star shivered to the uproar: the raucous howling of the spheres, the deep, incessant drumming of the cones. And, above all, the thunder of the gong, like the sobbing in unison of all the bells ever cast, a soul-chilling throb of alarm.

'Hasten, Giles,' urged Jay Kalam.

'Ah, Jay!' begged the old man, frantically. 'Have mercy!'

'You must,' the commander told him soberly. 'Or we shall die.'

And, as calmly as if he could not hear that hideous onslaught, Jay Kalam was still busy with the enigmatic mechanism in the long red case. Now he was fastening five wires to a binding post. Kay Nymidee, eagerly aiding

157

him, twisted one of the wires around Giles Habibula's fat arm. She made each of the others hold the end of a wire.

The gong still thundered its warning. Bob Star watched the monstrous throng come down, until he could see the pattern of the tread on the black belts of the spheres, see the multiple heads of the silent giants.

'I had hoped,' he heard Jay Kalam's calm voice, gravely regretful, 'that they would follow the ship, and give us time –'

Hal Samdu rumbled imploringly: 'Hurry, Giles!'

'In life's name,' gasped Giles Habibula. 'When I'm already dying –'

The foremost silver sphere was now close upon them. Its white tentacles whipped out toward Kay Nymidee. Bob Star set himself to leap at it in futile, bare-handed desperation.

'Wait!' breathed Jay Kalam.

He made some quick, final adjustment within the rectangular red case. A faint, momentary humming came from it, low at first, running up the scale of sound until it became ear-piercingly shrill, then inaudible. And it seemed to Bob Star that the light abruptly changed, as if a shadow had flickered across them. The nightmare throng was indefinably distorted; it appeared somehow withdrawn, as if seen through an inexplicable veil.

Besides that, he sensed nothing. But the white sphere jerked back its grasping tentacles. The alien horde was abruptly silent, as if with consternation. Monstrous things rebounded from the walls, retreating.

Beside him, Giles Habibula sighed deeply.

'Ah, me,' he gasped, with a vast relief. 'It's done!'

Wearily, he wiped his pale yellow face with the back of his hand. And Bob Star perceived that the entire bottom of the shaft had begun slipping away, like an enormously massive sliding door. A dark slit appeared at one side of the shaft, and widened. And presently they were looking down a great, square well, walled with jewel-smooth indigo, into another world, where a small green sun was shining, cold and dim.

Jay Kalam was the first to speak, his voice faint with awe.

'So this,' he said, 'is the hidden fortress of the Cometeers.'

Bob Star was amazed at the extent of the space beyond that mighty door. When they had pushed themselves through the shaft, and Giles Habibula had touched something that closed the vast barrier behind them, they all paused in a shuddering astonishment.

Bob Star's sense of directions had changed again, and it now seemed that this vast, dimly lit void was above them. It must have been fifty miles in diameter, he thought – perhaps five hundred. It was roughly spherical. The walls of it were partly wild cliffs of natural rock. And partly they were tremendous flat surfaces of that hard blue armour.

Machines loomed far away, in that twilit vastness, larger than any he had seen on the surface of the planet. They must be the engines, he thought, that ran upon the power of that captive sun to drive the clustered worlds of the comet like a ship. He felt that he could almost sense that flow of illimitable energy, and it gave him a sense of crushed futility.

It made him ill again. Suddenly he was clinging like a fly to the roof of his hollow world, and sick with the invincible fear that he was falling into the cold green sun at the centre of it. Then the green globe and the dim, cyclopean machines began to spin over and under him, over and under, until he shut his eyes, retching.

Faintly, he heard Kay Nymidee speaking, with awe and terror in her nervous voice, and the elation of a desperate daring.

'Kay says the weapon we seek is locked in the green sphere,' Jay Kalam interpreted. 'Two of the Cometeers, she says, are always stationed outside of it, on watch. Even those guards can't enter the sphere itself, for the metal of it is impregnated with forces that form a barrier to the energy-fields of their bodies. Only a few of the rulers of the comet are able to pass that barrier.'

'Kay and her father studied it with their projector, she says. But they were never able to penetrate the barrier. Kay doesn't know how to enter, or what may be within.'

Nauseated, trembling, Bob Star forced his eyes open. He peered uneasily at Kay Nymidee and the others – he dared not look again into that giddy void. Jay Kalam was gravely alert. Hal Samdu seemed grimly belligerent, but Giles Habibula was still greenishy ill.

'We must lose no time,' Jay Kalam went on decisively. 'The slaves are bewildered for the moment. But they saw the door open, and they'll report what happened. The Cometeers themselves won't be so easy to confuse. Somehow, we must reach the green globe.'

Bob Star stole an apprehensive glance at it – a small, dim green sun, far out in that sickening chasm of spinning emptiness.

'How can we get there?' he whispered. 'It's miles and miles away – and floating free –'

'Not floating,' Jay Kalam said. 'It must be suspended by those tubular fields. But still,' he admitted, 'there's nothing we can climb.'

'Then,' Bob Star whispered hopelessly, 'how –?'

The commander said quietly. 'We can jump.'

Bob Star gaped. 'Jump?'

'Certainly. There's no gravitation here to stop us. If we don't miss the globe, and go sailing on beyond –'

Instinctively, Bob Star's hands clutched at the railing beside the great door. Even the idea of a plunging fall through that directionless pit made him sick again. But Jay Kalam made them all crouch in a little circle upon the jewel-hard surface of the mighty door, holding hands. He had fastened the red, rectangular metal case to his belt, they all clung to the wires that ran from it

'When I give the word,' he said. 'we all jump toward the green sphere.'

To Bob Star, it began to spin again, over and under him. It took all his will to keep his eyes upon it. Dimly, he

heard the commander counting. He heard the quiet, 'Now!'
He leapt, with all his strength, into that dizzy gulf.

For a moment he was too ill to be aware of anything.
Then he knew that they were all clinging together, a helpless
little huddle of flying figures, drifting through the confused
vastness of a hollow world. The green sphere seemed
a very tiny and distant goal. And they were quite helpless
now to stop or turn.

'I'm afraid,' said Jay Kalam, 'that we're going to one
side.'

It was very strange, to Bob Star, to hear that voice, as
always cool and grave and perfectly modulated. A frightened whisper, a choking gasp, a scream, would have been in
better keeping with the nightmarish horror of that flight.
For the small green sun was whirling over and under them
again. All meaning and direction had vanished from the
vastness of that dim cavern. His sickness came back, made
intolerable by the lack of anything substantial to cling to.
He compressed his lips in silent agony.

'The damned Cometeers – these on guard?' he heard
Hal Samdu's booming question. 'Won't they see us?'

'Not so long as we hold these wires,' Jay Kalam answered.
'Though, of course, it's possible, they may detect us with
other senses than sight.'

Fighting his sickness, Bob Star looked along the glistening
red wire that he grasped, to the instrument at Jay Kalam's
belt.

'We aren't – ?' he gasped. 'We aren't – invisible?'

Sitting in empty space as calmly as if he rested in a
chair, the commander nodded soberly.

'Kay and I took the invisibility mechanism out of the
captured ship,' he said. 'In my haste to remove it, I got
it out of adjustment. We had some difficulty in discovering
the principle of it, so that we could repair it – our success
is due to Kay.

'It seems to create a special sort of energy-field around
objects electrically connected with it,' he explained. 'Light
rays striking one side of the field are absorbed, and instantly

reradiated from the other – as if they had gone straight through.'

'Then how can we see?' Bob Star asked. 'If there's no light inside?'

'That field, Kay says, has another effect. It absorbs other vibrations – apparently from the infrared end of the spectrum – and reradiates them as visible light, here inside the field, for the convenience of the user.'

'That's one danger,' the commander added softly. 'Though those slaves couldn't see us, Kay believes that the Cometeers themselves are sensitive to the infrared. If so, they will be able to see a shadow where we are –'

Another wave of illness swept away Bob Star's attention. During that fall – for to him it was a fall, through the giddy pit of some strange hell – time lost its meaning. He settled into a passive, agonized endurance. By turns, he opened and closed his eyes. He watched the dizzy spinning of that remote green sun, amid the monstrous mechanisms that drove the comet. He closed his eyes, and hung bathed in the silent eternal thunder of their power. And his illness did not cease.

With one hand he clung to Giles Habibula, who was still sick, green-faced and groaning. And he gripped the hand of Kay Nymidee. She was silent and pale, but sometimes, when he could see her face, she smiled a little. Time had seemed suspended. But at last Bob Star realized that the cold green ball was drawing near, but somewhat to one side. Jay Kalam was saying:

'Yes, we're about to miss it.'

'Ah, so,' sighed Giles Habibula. 'And it's my fault, Jay. I was too slow, when we jumped. Too weak with this mortal illness. I dragged you all aside –'

Bob Star shut his eyes, sick with defeat.

'Flying on by,' he muttered hopelessly. 'With no way to turn.'

He was amazed to hear Jay Kalam saying. 'But there is a way – at the cost of one of us.'

He whispered, 'How?'

162

'One of us,' the commander answered, 'must turn loose and kick away, so that the reaction will push us toward the globe. We are flying like a ship in space – and one of us must be the rocket.'

'That would work!' Bob Star exclaimed eagerly. Then dismay choked his voice to a whisper. 'But he would have to let go the wire, and leave the field. He would be visible again. And the Cometeers –'

'Aye, Jay,' Hal Samdu was rumbling, 'just tell me what to do.'

'No,' Bob Star protested quickly. 'I'll be the one –'

'Bob,' said the commander, quietly, 'you must stay with us.'

He gave Hal Samdu brief direction. And the giant crouched against the huddle of their drifting bodies, and then kicked powerfully away. His sprawling body spun through dim emptiness. It seemed to flicker, oddly, as it passed the veil of invisibility. It grew small, hurtling away into the greenish twilight.

Giles Habibula was abruptly sobbing, noisily. For a moment Bob Star felt the salt sting of tears in his own eyes, and an ache in his throat. But then he saw the pale, green ball again, almost upon them. And he gasped hoarsely:

'Look – there!'

For he had seen one of the shining guardians of the globe. A magnet of living light, with the red star and the violet for poles and the misty spindle between them like the field of a magnet turned to animate flame. It was more than alive. It was wondrous and beautiful and infinitely dreadful.

They drifted close to it – and it paused abruptly in its slow flight about the sphere. Bob Star's breath stopped. His skin felt cold with a sudden sweat, and his body tensed uselessly. He hung helpless in the air; there was nothing he could reach and nothing he could do.

For an instant the creature stood still. The pulsation of the bright stars ceased. And the misty spindle seemed frozen into a pillar of greenish ice. Then burning life returned. The Cometeer darted away, in the direction Hal Samdu had gone.

'It was Hal who it saw,' Jay Kalam whispered. 'But it will soon be looking for us.'

A moment later, they thudded against the cold, hard metal of the faintly glowing sphere. They crouched upon it, held by a slight attraction. More like an asteroid than the green sun it had first appeared to be, it was, Bob Star thought, perhaps half a mile in diameter.

Kay Nymidee was whispering swiftly to Jay Kalam.

'She says the weapon is inside,' he interpreted quietly. 'This ball is a kind of safe.'

'Ah, so!' gasped Giles Habibula. 'And what a safe!'

Chapter Eighteen

AT THE EMPTY BOX

Every safe, Jay Kalam reasoned, must have a door. They searched, shuffling very carefully across the coldly glowing metal, walking by the aid of its slight gravitation. At last they came to a square, twenty-foot depression, surrounded by a low metal flange.

Giles Habibula scrambled down into the pit, and examined a triple circle of projecting metal rods.

'Ah, me!' he moaned with dismay. 'If that last lock was difficult, this one is impossible. The masters of the comet couldn't open it themselves, with all their precious science, if ever they lost the combination. What a lock! You could try possible combinations at random till the universe runs down, and the odds are a million to one the door would still be closed.'

His thick fingers, so uncannily sensitive, so amazingly deft, were already swiftly busy, sliding the rods in and out, twirling them. Intently he was listening, although Bob Star could hear no faintest sound.

The others clung to the flange above him. Bob Star, at intervals, was still actutely ill. And momentarily he expected to see the dread, shining pillar of one of the Cometeers materialize beside him, perhaps to speak with the triumphant voice of Stephen Orco.

Urgently, Jay Kalam inquired at last, 'Can't you do it, Giles!'

The old man looked up, to wipe sweat from his sick yellow face with the back of his hand. He shook his head. 'It's a fearful test of my genius, Jay. Never was such a lock built in the System. The emperors of the comet must not trust their own guards.'

Wearily, he bent again.

'Opening locks,' he muttered absently, 'is largely a matter of point of view. To any of you, a lock is something to prevent the opening of a door – and it does prevent it. But old Giles sees a lock as a means of opening the door – and it is.'

He groaned, and spat.

'Or at least,' he amended, 'it should be. But old Giles never met such a lock as this.'

Kay Nymidee had seized Jay Kalam's arm, to whisper frantically.

'Hasten, Giles,' he pleaded. 'Kay says they'll surely find us soon. Our invisibility, remember, is a trick of their own. It can't baffle them long.'

The old man looked up again, his small red eyes round with unexpected anger.

'For life's sake,' he burst out, 'have you no patience?

'Here is Giles Habibula, a feeble old soldier, faint and retching in his last illness, dying far from home. Ah, so, a dying man, taxing his genius to the last precious ounce, to solve a riddle that would baffle all the scientists and mathematicians and doddering philosophers in the System for the next thousand years!

'In the name of precious life, can't you let him work in peace, without screaming in his ear –'

'Forgive me, Giles,' the commander begged hastily. 'I'm sorry. Go on.'

The old man shook his head, muttering, and bent again to the triple circle of projecting rods. His deft hands paused at last, and a faint vibration whispered through the faintly glowing metal. The floor of the pit began to slip aside, and Giles Habibula scrambled hastily for the flange at the edge.

'A desperate trial!' he gasped. 'But the door is open –'

Bob Star crept forward to watch the widening slit, which revealed a deep, square well, walled with coldly shining metal. The way was open, to the weapon that could kill Stephen Orco! That triumphant thought swept him forward eagerly – and then halted him, with smashing agony.

For he couldn't kill Stephen Orco. He couldn't kill anybody. He had been trying to think that he was slowly conquering that crippling obsession – until the battle to take the prison-ship, when the organic ray from that cone-shaped creature stabbed into his head. But its merciless thrust had brought back all the torture of the Iron Confessor – he wondered dully now if that orange-coloured ray had carried an ultrasonic component that acted on the same pain centres of the brain. Whatever the effect, it had speeded the merciless beat of that old pain, and reinforced that imperative injunction.

He couldn't kill –

'Come on,' Jay Kalam was urging. 'We've no time to spare.'

They pushed themselves into the square pit. Hundreds of feet they dropped, aided now by the feeble gravitation of the metal sphere, and struck another door, studded with three more circles of projecting rods.

'Another lock,' muttered Giles Habibula. 'But now I know the principle.'

He touched something, and the first door closed ponderously behind them. He bent to the second lock.

'Never,' he wheezed abstractedly, 'was my genius so fearfully tried. And never fired by such dire emergency! Ah, me! this day will mark the death of Giles Habibula! This monstrous safe may well become his tomb.'

The shining metal murmured again, and the enormous mass of the inner door slipped aside. They followed the square passage on beyond, into a small, square room which must have been near the centre of the sphere. It was flooded with the greenish radiation of the walls, and the passage behind them was the only entrance.

The little chamber was empty, save for a massive, rectangular box of the scarlet metal, three feet long, fixed to the inner wall. Its sides were covered with intricate heiroglyphic designs in silver and black. Upon the top of it was another triple circle of projecting rods.

Moaning under his breath, Giles Habibula applied himself.

As the inner door, also, closed behind them, Bob Star clung to the glowing wall, regarding the box with a certain incredulous awe. Already he was a little disappointed. His vague expectations had included something more impressive than this red chest, so small that one man might almost have carried it.

'It's no use,' he whispered. 'No use!'

For what manner of weapon, hidden in so small a space, could defeat the tremendous science whose awe-compelling evidences had surrounded them so long?

He went cold and rigid with alarm when another vibration whispered through the palely shining metal. Kay Nymidee began to tremble. From her white, drawn lips came a strained, unconscious little cry.

'The outer door,' Jay Kalam whispered. 'They are coming.'

'Ah!' gasped Giles Habibula. 'Here! It's open!'

Bob Star sprang apprehensively to his side, to help throw back the lid of the scarlet box. He hardly knew what he had expected to find. He couldn't imagine what might destroy that shining thing which now held the mind of Stephen Orco. He peered anxiously into the box, and his jaw fell slack upon a voiceless cry of dismay.

For it was empty.

For a moment he felt numb and faint with consternation. Intolerable vertigo came back. He was shaken with painful, futile retchings. The green walls of the small, square room spun about him. Quivering cold with sweat, he clung to the edge of the empty box.

'Jay, it's all in vain,' he heard Giles Habibula's weary murmur. 'There's nothing – ' The old man's breath went out, with a hopeless sigh. 'Ah, me!' he wheezed. 'Never did fate perpetrate such a fearful jest!'

'Never did men ever struggle so, for no reward at all.' His bald head shook sadly. 'We roved the frozen night of Neptune's polar desert to find a ship, and fought a mad cannibal for it. We voyaged the perilous wastes of space, until the shining monster met us. We dwelt amid the haunting horror of the asteroid, and entered the terror of the comet upon it. We plunged close to death in that atomic furnace. We took that ship, when they tried to make cattle of us, and came fifteen thousand miles upon it, into the core of an armoured planet. We worked locks that were fearful difficult, and made our bodies into a living ship of space – ah, poor Hal, who perished for us! Now old Giles Habibula has exhausted his precious well of genius, to break into the strongest safe in all the universe.

'But all in vain. The thing is empty – '

Sobs choked his voice.

Moved by a thought that the weapon might be really in the box, perhaps concealed by another invisibility-device, Bob Star groped for it hopefully. His searching fingers found only hard bare metal. With a helpless shrug, he looked up at Jay Kalam and Kay Nymidee.

Ghostly white, the girl was staring down into the empty box. Her bloodless face had gone flaccid with despair. Her eyes were wide, dull with the death of hope. Her body looked limp, nerveless – he thought she would have fallen, had there been gravitation to make anything fall.

Jay Kalam, was rigid and silent, ashen-faced. Though he somehow had kept his expression of grave composure, it had no meaning. His eyes were blank windows into vacant space, with no light in them. His lean, slender fingers were twisted together, with a mute agony.

The girl's dull eyes crossed Bob Star's, without warmth or recognition. She began talking as if to herself, in a dead, husky whisper. Jay Kalam interpreted her words, but it seemed to Bob Star that he did so like an automatic machine, without himself comprehending anything.

'I am the last of my people. For twelve generations we have dwelt inside the comet. We have survived through times when death would have been welcome, for one thing – to destroy the Cometeers before they could destroy mankind. My father lived and died for that, and all my people did. Now at last I thought we had a chance. But we have lost – '

His voice grew slow, and faded away, as if he had been a machine running down. Giles Habibula was still slumped over the empty box. He was weeping noisily, blowing his nose. His fat fingers were restlessly exploring the smooth red metal, in aimless search.

Straightening convulsively, Bob Star whispered, 'Can't we do – anything?'

Jay Kalam shook his head. His teeth had cut his lip, and his lean chin was bright with blood. The grave restraint of his face made a strange contrast with that scarlet stain. He shook his head and licked his lip, and seemed dully surprised at the taste of blood.

'We can only wait, now – for them – '

Dazed, hopeless, Bob Star stared vacantly into the empty box. They had failed, and they were doomed. The old pain beat stronger and faster against his brain. The ancient fear seized him; it would never die.

Sickness came back. He crumpled down beside moaning Giles Habibula, in trembling, agonized despair. He scarcely heard the remote whisper of the inner door, opening, but the dry and voiceless gasp of Kay Nymidee drew up his eyes.

He saw the Cometeers.

Two of them, dropping into that small green room. Out of the nearer pillar of bright mist came a low chuckle of careless triumph. It was the reckless laugh of a mocking god. Listening dully in his apathy, Bob Star heard the familiar, ringing baritone of Stephen Orco:

'Greetings, Bob. Allow me to present my colleague, who is the nominal ruler of the comet.'

The violet star dipped slightly, as if it had made a mocking bow.

With a certain dim, lethargic interest, Bob Star stared at the shining lord of the comet. It, he supposed, was responsible for the monstrous joke of the empty box. Were the Cometeers, he wondered, indeed completely invulnerable? Had this tremendous, guarded vault been but a fantastic hoax, designed to support the authority of this shining emperor?

'Your remarkable enterprise,' the easy voice of Stephen Orco continued, 'has alarmed my colleague, who is going to take steps for its immediate termination. I regret your untimely passing, Bob, but your outrageous indiscretions have made it impracticable for me to preserve your life any longer.'

If the voice had gibbered or whispered or shrieked, Bob Star thought, the horror of it would have been easier to bear. For there was a dreadful discrepancy between the terrible burning wonder that spun before his eyes, and that careless tone of laughing levity.

'Before you die, Bob, wouldn't you like to hear of your parents? They are quite near, you know – so near that your unfortunate companion, Hal Samdu, was brought upon his capture to their prison-ship. That is how I came to be aware of your extraordinary activities.

'Your mother, you will doubtless be relieved to know, is yet uninjured. But she has been displaying a foolish and useless reluctance to enter any discussion with me of the principles of AKKA – a reluctance which is soon to have a festive end. I had planned for you and your companions to be present at the banquet. But the impatience of my imperial colleague puts that out of the question.'

There was a little pause, and Bob Star observed an anxious, restless movement of the misty pillar spinning within the thing that was master of the comet.

'It is a pleasure,' resumed the brightly sardonic voice of Stephen Orco, 'to be present at a crisis in universal history. And, as I interpret the somewhat apprehensive behaviour of my colleague, as we entered, this is indeed a crisis. I believe that your audacious indiscretion in forcing your way into the chamber of generation is going to result in an order for the immediate total extermination of mankind. A somewhat solemn occasion, don't you agree?'

An untroubled chuckle rang from that column of living light.

'Not that I'm going to feel any compunction about assisting with the execution –'

171

The bright shape of the ruler of the Cometeers had moved again, as if impatiently. A shadowy arm of that bright haze reached out – and Bob Star felt a tingling of his skin. A greenish mist began to blur his vision. This, he thought, was the ultimate moment.

'Wait, Orco!'

Dimly, through the sudden rushing in his deafened ears, Bob Star heard Jay Kalam's strained and husky voice.

'Wait – if you want to know how you can assist so calmly with the extermination of mankind. Because I can tell you why, Stephen Orco. I know who – what – you really are.'

Bob Star was aware of reprieve. The tingling numbness receded from his limbs. He could see again, and the roaring faded from his ears. He heard the mocking challenge of Stephen Orco's voice:

'Well, Commander Kalam?'

Jay Kalam paused as if to choose his words, and spoke at last with a strangely cool deliberation.

'Stephen Orco,' he said, 'we first tried to enter the comet upon a small geodesic cruiser. A shining monster came aboard; it wrecked our generators and killed an old associate of yours, one Mark Lardo.'

'I am aware of the incident – none better,' Orco's voice cut in impatiently.

Listening, Bob Star wondered vaguely at the commander's purpose. He was fighting for time, obviously. Yet what, in this ultimate extremity of defeat, was the value of time? In a moment, however, is wonder was lost, in his consuming interest in Jay Kalam's revelation.

'We landed the wreck upon an uncharted transplutonian asteroid. It had been inhabited. Its people had been destroyed by the Cometeers. They left us a fascinating mystery. A thousand things told us that the owner of the asteroid had been an able scientist and a gifted artist. Everything on that tiny world proclaimed his genius – and his amazing wealth. It was hard for us to imagine why such a man should have hidden himself on that lonely rock, outside the System.'

172

'But why is your problem of any interest to me?' inquired the voice from that shining thing.

'Because it explains your difference from other men,' Jay Kalam said. 'Your unusual gifts, your desire for superiority, your hostility to mankind.'

'Go on,' said Orco's voice. 'But be quick.'

And it seemed to Bob Star that the nearer shining thing made a restraining gesture, to halt some act of the ruler of the comet.

'One remarkable feature of the riddle,' the commander continued, 'was a very complete biological laboratory, cleverly hidden beneath the dwelling. Another was the emblem that strange exile had chosen to mark his belongings – the *crux ansata* and crossed bones, in red, on a black background. You may recall that the same emblem – the symbol of life above the symbol of death – is associated with the puzzle of your own origin?'

The shining being came a little nearer; the restless whirling of its green-and-argent pillar seemed to pause; Bob Star sensed its compelling interest.

'When the asteroid was dragged into the comet –'

'Thank you.' The bright being chuckled. 'Your penetration of the outer barrier had perplexed my new associates. But go on.'

'The asteroid was flung into that power plant,' Jay Kalam continued. 'But not before I had solved its riddle. The exile,' he explained, 'kept a diary in a secret shorthand, which I was able to read.' He paused to shake his head, at Bob Star's stifled gasp of unbelief. 'What I read,' he went on soberly, 'I have kept to myself until now – because of its unpleasant aspects.'

'Let's have it,' rapped the voice from the pillar of light. 'My colleague will not submit to much longer restraint.'

'That fantastic exile,' the commander went on, still deliberately grave – 'was a man named Eldo Arrynu. A native of Earth, he was educated there and on Mars in biological science. Eldo Arrynu was peculiarly brilliant, in artistic as well as scientific directions. His early career was distinguished, until he was sentenced in disgrace to a Martian prison for conducting illegal biological experiments.'

Jay Kalam paused to get his breath – still fighting, Bob Star realized, for time.

'Within a year after his imprisonment, he was pardoned, in reward for a brilliant emergency operation that saved the warden's life. He vanished. And the Legion was never able to find him again – although we had evidence enough of his diabolical activities.

'What he did, of course, was to take refuge upon this uncharted asteroid. In prison, apparently he had formed connections with a powerful ring of space pirates and interplanetary smugglers, who had used it as a base. He soon became the leader of the ring, evidently, and turned its criminal activities in a new and terrible direction.

'On that asteroid, he became the source of the most insidious traffic that has ever disgraced the System, one the Legion has fought in vain to suppress. It's the profits of that monstrous traffic that transformed a barren rock into a hidden paradise – '

'Be brief,' warned the voice of Stephen Orco. 'Or die.'

'The illegal experiments of Eldo Arrynu,' Jay Kalam continued, still gravely unhurried, 'had been in the synthesis of life – the grisly consequences of such efforts long ago forced the council to outlaw them. Working on that asteroid, Arrynu carried his forbidden work to a triumphant completion. The business that brought him such enormous wealth was the manufacture and sale of androids.'

For a moment the nearer shining thing seemed frozen. Red star and violet star ceased their regular beat. And the misty spindle between them was congealed into a pillar of green-white crystal. Then it broke into quivering motion, and one startled word came out of it:

'Androids!'

'Eldo Arrynu,' amplified Jay Kalam, 'had come upon the secret of synthetic life. He generated artificial cells, and propagated them in nutrient media, and learned how to control their development by radiological and biochemical means.

'He was an artist, as well as a scientist. The genius of creation must have possessed him. The medium of his great art was living, synthetic flesh. He achieved miracles – diabolical miracles – '

The commander's lean face had grown dark and hard, as if with the pain of a festering memory.

'It is a sorry commentary upon human civilization,' he said grimly, 'that a wealthy man should give half his fortune for a hundred pounds of synthetic protoplasm. But many did – enough to give Eldo Arrynu the wealth he desired.'

His hard jaws clenched suddenly, until they went pale.

'Nor can I blame them, altogether,' he whispered. His dark eyes seemed to stare into a terrible window of the past. 'For there was one, arrested by the Legion for her owner's murder. She was the spirit of beauty, made real; she was a true artist's dream of grace. To look at, she was the very soul of womanly innocence. To listen to, her golden voice – '

His lean throat worked to a convulsive swallow.

'It became my duty to destroy her. But – almost – ' His dark eyes looked suddenly, gratefully, at Bob Star. 'But for the memory of your mother, Bob, I might have brought disgrace upon the Legion – '

He collected himself, and his eyes swept back to the restless shining forms.

'The criminal activities of the ring did not stop with the mere sale of the androids,' he said. 'Because the flawless, enthralling perfection of their bodies frequently concealed the most unspeakable evil. The luckless purchaser of their matchless loveliness often found that the price included the remainder of his fortune, even if not his life.

'Eldo Arrynu wrote black pages into the records of the Legion – '

'But,' the commander went on, 'if he failed to provide his creations with any moral restraints, Eldo Arrynu seems to have had no difficulty in endowing them with extraordinary cunning – or even, sometimes, with an exceptional intelligence.'

Jay Kalam paused momentarily, and continued almost casually:

'You must already have guessed what I'm about to tell you, Stephen Orco. You aren't a man. You are a synthetic monster from the laboratory of Eldo Arrynu.'

The frozen violet star dipped as if it had bowed. The sardonic voice of Stephen Orco spoke out of the misty pillar, ringing as if with a careless amusement:

'Thank you, Commander.'

'Your case,' Jay Kalam went on, 'is fully discussed in the diary. Eldo Arrynu took exceptional pains with your creation. His sublime artistic genius must have got the better, temporarily, of his practical business instincts. He designed you to be a perfect being, a true superman.

'Soon, however, after you emerged from his vats and incubators, he perceived the fatal flaw in you – the cold fiend, sleeping. He saw that his supreme effort had fallen far short of humanity, in the most vital direction possible.

'The diary records a curious struggle. One entry praises your physical perfection and your remarkable intelligence; it glows with his love for you – for he did love you, with the absorption of an artist in his masterpiece, and the devotion of a man for his son.

'The next entry, however, is a gloomy record of doubts and misgivings, filled with evidences of the fiendish coldness that all Arrynu's arts could never eradicate from you. It ends with determination to destroy you.

'Unfortunately, however, that strange exile could never quite bring himself to the task. His love and his well-founded fear drove him at last into a regrettable compromise. He sealed you into a magnelithium cylinder, with everything necessary to preserve your life, and cast you adrift in space, far from the asteroid.

'By concealing his identity from you,' said the commander solemnly, 'he hoped to escape the consequences of his folly. But even so, you destroyed your own maker, Stephen Orco, when you loosed the Cometeers upon the system.

'It's possible that your long, helpless confinement in the

cylinder had some farther adverse influence in the formation of a character that was never good. Some part of your insatiable appetite for power and superiority must be by way of compensation for that imprisonment.

'But you were never human –'

'I'm grateful, Commander,' Stephen Orco's voice broke in, carelessly mocking as ever. 'But I fail to perceive any advantage to you in revealing my origins. Certainly, it isn't going to make me any more generous to the human cattle on which I feed, to know that I was never one of them.'

The bright mist chuckled.

'If you expected gratitude –'

The voice paused abruptly, as the shining ruler of the Cometeers made an imperative forward motion, and then it added quickly:

'Now you may prepare to die.'

Chapter Nineteen

THE MAN WHO BROKE

Listening to the Commander's quietly spoken narrative, staring at the luminous and beautiful thing that was now Stephen Orco, Bob Star had been shaken with a savage conflict of strange emotions.

For his great enemy had never been anything more human than this thing of frozen fire! That fact explained part of the fear and hatred that had twisted and smothered him ever since that dreadful night at the academy. It was no man that had driven the dull blade of the Iron Confessor into his skull, but a thing already inhuman.

With that knowledge, the pulse of pain behind that old scar seemed to weaken and waver in its beat, for the first time in nine years. He dared again to feel that he might somehow find strength to defy the crippling command that Orco's transformed voice had burned into his brain. His empty hands tightened, hungry for a weapon.

He was crouching beside the empty box. Old Giles Habibula was still bent over it, clinging to the sides of it when the waves of retching shook him, still sobbing noisily and frequently blowing his nose.

'Now you may prepare to die.' The hurried final words of Stephen Orco seemed to echo in his mind. 'Because my imperial colleague seems peculiarly apprehensive about your presence in the chamber of generation – '

Bob Star felt the slight, unobtrusive pressure of the old man's trembling arm against his side, and then the cold weight of the small object Giles Habibula pressed into his hand. A light of understanding burst over him; he knew why the commander had wanted time.

Turning to shield the object with his body, he stole a quick glance at it. A puzzling weapon – if it were a weapon. A polished cube of some hard black stuff, not quite two inches on an edge. Its surface had the cold, soapy slickness of a polished gem. It felt oddly heavy – though it was weightless now, he could feel the inertia of its mass. Projecting from one face was a red, knurled knob.

Clutching it, Bob Star tried not to show his abrupt, breathless tension. It must be the weapon – and he knew that he himself must use it, instantly. The attention of Stephen Orco and the ruler of the Cometeers was probably still on the commander. That might give him time to strike.

But he couldn't kill –

Or – could he? For one frozen moment, as his quivering fingers closed on that harmless-looking instrument, it seemed to him that he was back in that dark basement room at the academy museum, nine years ago. The rusty metal band of the Iron Confessor was around his head again, and that three-edged blade driven once more into his skull, with Stephen Orco's taunting voice vibrating from it in waves of ultimate agony.

'So you don't like it, pup? This rusty crown of your proud forefathers! But no matter how little you like it, you'll never do anything about it. Because this ingenious little device was made to break men. You may be able to defy your conscience and the law, or even to forget your honour as an officer of the Legion, but you'll never disobey the Iron Confessor.

'And you can't kill me, Bob. You can't kill –'

His trembling fingers had relaxed to drop the black cube, because he couldn't use it. But then Kay Nymidee must have glimpsed it, for he heard her catch her breath. The bright image of her flashed into his mind, and his surge of tortured emotion swept him back again to that dark room.

He could feel the sticky pull of his own seeping blood drying on his face, and taste its salt sweetness on his lips. Once more he saw the wild rage on Orco's handsome face, dim in the glow from the tubes of the Iron Confessor. He heard the tramp of the night watchman's feet, in the corridor above, and then the whispered voices of Orco's friends.

Those things had been forgotten, buried beneath his fear and pain. The footsteps and those protesting voices – frightened and defiant, when he heard them now. Hazing was in the academy tradition, but this thing had gone too far. If Bob Star died, the truth would certainly come out. Murder. All Stephen Orco's cleverness wouldn't be enough to save them from court-martial.

But Orco had grown too angry to listen to them.

'Say it, pup!' That dreadful voice came flooding through Bob Star's brain again, transformed to red agony by the vibration of that three-edged blade. Once more it repeated all the unspeakable lies that Orco wanted him to swear. And again it insisted, mercilessly, 'Say it, pup.'

But he had never said it.

'He has got you beaten, Orco.' Now he heard those other voices, sharpened with increasing fear as the watchman's steady footfalls paused in the corridor. 'You can't break him – not even with the Iron Confessor. Don't you know he's John Star's son?'

The buried truth came rushing back.

'I give up!' Those long-forgotten words were Stephen Orco's – and the hush of fear had swept the rasping anger from his voice. 'He's tougher than I expected. Let's get him out of here – and fix up a story for him. He's John Star's son, remember. Too proud to go telling tales.

'Aren't you, pup?' Stephen Orco had turned to speak into that cruel device again, before they removed it. 'You'll forget it, won't you, pup?'

For nine years, he had forgotten.

All that came flashing through his mind, while he clutched that cold black cube. He was John Star's son – and Stephen Orco had been the one who broke. Somehow, his fingers were suddenly steady. He lifted the cube, twisting at that tiny scarlet knob.

A pale beam of silver light shone from the opposite face of

the cube. He twisted the little instrument, to sweep that beam towards the shining things.

'Bob! You can't – '

But he could. That startled, apprehensive outcry became a harsh scream. It faded into a bubbling note of ultimate agony – which might have come from a dying victim of the Iron Confessor.

His glance had followed that beam of silver light. Even before it struck those two shining beings, they seemed to freeze. For an instant they hung motionless. Their radiance died. They became two ghostly wisps of pale grey dust. The dust swirled, and then there was nothing.

Stephen Orco and the emperor of the Cometeers were dead.

The green walls rushed away from Bob Star, and time seemed to pause. For an instant his very victory was somehow appalling, because it had shattered the whole orientation of his life. But then he knew that the old throb of pain had died behind that scar – perhaps. Jay Kalam later suggested, the painful thrust of that organic ray had somehow helped erase the marks of the Iron Confessor.

The cold walls came back, and he heard the glad little sob of Kay Nymidee. An eager smile had swept the shadows of ominous foreboding from her face, for the first time since he had known her. She was suddenly in his arms, almost hysterical at first, and then happily relaxed.

Wonderingly, Jay Kalam picked up the black cube, which Bob Star had dropped back into the empty box. It had become covered with feathery crystals of frost. He brushed them away, and tried the red knob again. Nothing happened.

'It seems to be dead,' he said. 'Exhausted.'

'Perhaps I turned the knob too far,' Bob Star said. 'The thing seemed to kick back in my hands. I think the mass of it decreased. It was growing very cold, before I dropped it.'

The commander nodded, watching the white frost come back.

'I suspect,' he said thoughtfully, 'that you released a great deal of energy, of some sort that we can't perceive – ' He caught his breath. 'Did you notice?' His low voice had quickened, with more emotion than he often showed. 'Both those creatures were stricken – or seemed to be – before the white ray touched them!'

'Huh?' Bob Star peered at the mass of glittering frost, and back at the commander's grave face. 'Do you think – '

'A very little of that energy was enough to kill these two.' Jay Kalam's lean finger scraped at the dark stubble on his blood-stained chin. 'We don't know how. But Orco told us the Cometeers were stable fields of energy. Perhaps this instrument generated some key vibration, adjusted to destroy that stability. If that is so – and if the range of this weapon is as great as it should have been to enforce the authority of that shining emperor – then I imagine that we have won a very decisive victory.'

Deftly juggling the frosty cube, he replaced it in the box.

'Where did you get it?' he asked Giles Habibula. 'We thought the box was empty.'

'Ah, so it was.' The old soldier blew his nose again. His fat hands still clung to the box, his pudgy fingers caressing the oddly intricate designs on its sides. His illness had vanished.

'Then,' Bob Star whispered, 'how – ?'

'This pattern was the key,' wheezed Giles Habibula. 'It made me wonder from the beginning, for the makers of this safe had wasted none of their cunning on useless ornament anywhere else. The figures of it led my fingers to a hidden lock. The combination rods are set level with the surface – to make the black circles in the design. I had just found it, when those fearful creatures came upon us. I gave Jay a signal to distract them, while I set out to open it.

'Mortal me!' He shuddered. 'The precious genius of Giles Habibula could never endure another such trial. His poor old heart would stop. As it was, death was breathing on him when he found the combination – and saw that queer device lying where there had been nothing!'

'Where had it been?' Bob Star asked. 'Under a false bottom, do you think?'

'Nothing so simple!' Giles Habibula shook his head. 'I can see through false bottoms, blindfolded. Life knows where it was!' He peered at the commander. 'What do you think, Jay?'

Reflectively, Jay Kalam rubbed his chin.

'The Cometeers knew more of space and time than we do,' he said slowly. 'Their tubular force-fields are evidence of that as their own bodies were. That weapon may have been hidden somewhere across our universe, linked to a field that would draw it back when the lock was worked. Or it may have been outside our frame of space and time altogether – such a thing would not have been impossible for them.'

'It's lucky you had read that diary,' Bob Star looked up at him, frowning. 'But still I wonder why they let you delay them so long. When the ruler of the Cometeers found us here so near his secret, I wonder why he didn't kill us instantly.'

'I was wondering, while I was talking to Orco.' The commander nodded gravely. 'And I've a guess to offer. I don't think the shining emperor had been quite frank with his new ally. Orco seems to have been allowed to believe that his wonderful new body was entirely invulnerable. And you recall that he referred to this place as the chamber of generation – he had probably been deceived about the nature of the secret guarded here. I suspect that the ruler of the Cometeers kept quiet about the weapon, holding it in reserve to counter Orco's knowledge of AKKA.

'If that's the way it was, Orco must have been quite confident of his new-found immortality, and free of any alarm, until the end. His imperial companion was obviously apprehensive, and impatient to be done with us. But, in such circumstances, he would have been unable to take any very precipitate action without the danger that Orco would find out the truth – and the Cometeers have a new emperor –'

Jay Kalam was interrupted by a bulky missile that came plunging down the square well of the entrance, and thudded heavily against the coldly glowing metal. It gasped for breath, and straightened, and became the body of Hal

Samdu. It still bore the marks of battle, but joyous blue eyes were shining through the reddened bandages.

'Aye, Bob,' the giant rumbled. 'I told your mother you would be here.'

'My mother?' Bob Star whispered. 'Is she – safe?'

'Aye,' said Hal Samdu. 'She's waiting on that saucership, outside. And your father, too. The strange slaves of the Cometeers are all around them, but you needn't mind them now. They're our friends, now that we have killed their shining masters – '

'The Cometeers?' Jay Kalam broke in. 'How many did we kill?'

'Every one,' boomed the bandaged man. 'So John Star has learned from the slaves. I don't know what you did, but the slaves are rejoicing because the monsters are all destroyed, out to the limits of the comet.'

'I had begun to hope so.' Jay Kalam's dark eyes fell to the small black cube, which looked more than ever harmless now, with the film of frost thawing from it. 'Yet I scarcely dared – '

Hal Samdu's great hand caught Bob Star's arm.

'Come, Bob,' he said, 'to your mother.'

John Star was waiting at the entrance valve, to welcome them to the ship. His hard body looked trim and soldierly as ever in the green of the Legion. Bob Star was secretly amazed when his father kissed him. And a lump came up in his own throat when John Star called him, for the first time in many years, not Robert, but Bob.

They entered the ship, and climbed to the upper deck. Far back, beyond the central dome, were ranked a score of the strange slaves of the Cometeers: silvery globes, slim green cone-shaped things, lank, many-limbed red giants. The creatures stood motionless and silent, and Bob Star could sense their awe of these insignificant bipeds, who had wiped out their shining masters – an awe that had good cause, now that Stephen Orco was dead, and Aladoree's weapon effective once more.

She came to meet them, walking with the light, quick

184

grace he remembered. Even in the gloom of this hollow world, her brown hair shone with reddish glints and her cool grey eyes were luminous with joy. Rejoicing to the comfortable pull of the ship's gravity cells, which swept away his lingering vertigo, Bob Star ran to take her in his arms.

'My son!' She kissed him, laughing. 'You've grown a frightful beard!'

She embraced Jay Kalam and Giles Habibula, who long ago had been her bodyguards. And then Bob Star presented Kay Nymidee, with his arm around her waist.

'Mother, here's a stranger. She's alone. All her people were murdered by the Cometeers. She doesn't speak much English – but she will, soon. I want you to make her welcome. For it was she who showed us where to find the weapon that killed the Cometeers. And because – because I love her.'

Kay whispered something, softly, smiling at his mother. His mother took his hand, and hers, and put them together. Kay laughed a little, her fingers squeezing his, and suddenly he was longing to be with her in the peaceful beauty of the gardens of Phobos, which would no longer be a prison to him now.

'I'm glad, Bob,' his mother was whispering. 'Glad – '

She paused, and they listened to his father's crisp voice:

'– then, Jay, what can we do with the comet?'

'There are, I believe, three possible alternatives,' the commander answered thoughtfully. 'The keeper of the peace may be requested to destroy the entire comet – an irrational action, which I still oppose. Or it may be kept and governed as a permanent part of the System. Or the liberated slaves, if they are capable of operating it, may be allowed to depart with it. I should prefer the third choice, but of course the final decision is a matter for the Council.

'In any case, the comet offers us a magnificent accession of knowledge.' His grave eyes shone with a quick enthusiasm. 'I'm already planning to return immediately, as soon as we have safely returned the keeper of the peace to the

185

Purple Hall. I want to bring teams of experts in every branch of learning – '

Bob Star felt very tired, and the commander's ringing voice began to matter less than the warmth of Kay's arm against him. Faintly, as if from some vast distance, he heard the plaintive whine of Giles Habibula:

'Come along, Hal, and let's see if we can't find some proper human food and drink – '

Also available in Sphere Books

DAMNATION ALLEY
Roger Zelazny

Winner of both the Hugo and Nebula
Awards, Roger Zelazny has created in
Damnation Alley a terrifying story of an
odyssey through man-made hell. Damnation
Alley is three thousand miles of radio-active
wasteland, torn by hurricanes and fire
storms, the domain of mutants and
monsters. Hell Tanner, the last Angel to
survive from the Big Raid which destroyed
most of America, is the only man with a
chance to cross from California with the
plague serum desperately needed in Boston.
Damnation Alley lay directly in his path.

0 7221 94250   60p

Now a major Twentieth Century Fox
release, starring Jan-Michael Vincent,
George Peppard and Dominique Sanda.

SOLDIER, ASK NOT

On New Earth, the black-clad mercenaries
of the Friendly planets pitted their religious
fanaticism against the cold courage of the
Dorsai. Playing one against the other was
Tam Olyn, who, in his search to avenge his
dead brother-in-law, was ready to use his
frightening knowledge of the Final
Encyclopaedia.

0 7221 2952 1   60p

DORSAI!

Donal Graeme, Dorsai of the Dorsai, was
the ultimate soldier, a master of space war
and strategy. With Donal at their head, the
Dorsai embarked upon the final, seemingly
impossible venture: unification of the
splintered worlds of Mankind.

0 7221 2951 3   50p

More Great Science Fiction Authors
from Sphere

WAR OF THE WING-MEN
Poul Anderson

A sci-fi adventure classic from Hugo
Award-winning author Poul Anderson.
When three Terrans crash-landed on
Diomedes it was clear that their supplies
would not carry them across the thousands
of miles of unmapped territory to the one
Terran outpost. Their only hope was help
from the Wing-Men, the barbarian
inhabitants of Diomedes.

0 7221 1161 4   60p

THE FALL OF THE TOWERS
Samuel R. Delaney

A saga of stunning imaginative power from
the winner of three Nebula Awards. The
Empire of Toromon was the last hope of
mankind after the Great Fire. Sealed off
from the radioactive wastelands, the Empire
survived to face new and deadly adversaries
– the Lord of the Flames, the berserk
Imperial military computer, and an
invading alien intelligence in search of
conquest.

0 7221 2899 1   50p

More Great Science Fiction Authors
from Sphere

THE WORLD OF NULL-A
A. E. Van Vogt

Gosseyn himself didn't know his own
identity – only that he could be killed, yet
live again. But someone knew who Gosseyn
was, and was using him as a pawn in a
deadly game that spanned the galaxy!

0 7221 8757 2   45p

THE PAWNS OF NULL-A
A. E. Van Vogt

Gosseyn knew the creature threatened to
destroy the whole solar system, but not
even his Null-A-trained double brain could
thwart the Follower's plans. Then he found
himself face-to-face with a force that lay
at the very roots of human intelligence . . .
all the while fighting his own insane mind.

0 7221 8772 6   45p